THE WARRIOR TEENS

AARAV WAGHMARE

Made with ♥ on the Notion Press Platform
www.notionpress.com

To all the young writers who believe

they can take their readers to

a whole new world.

Contents

Preface

Hello, I'm Aarav Waghmare, the author of this book. Through these pages, you'll join Krish and his friends as they narrate an intriguing tale filled with adventure, action, and excitement. Their journey promises to captivate your imagination and keep you hooked from start to finish. I hope you enjoy every twist and turn of their story.

Acknowledgements

Writing my first book has been an incredible journey, and I am deeply grateful to the many people who supported, guided, and inspired me along the way. I would like to give my heartfelt thanks, in particular, to my dad, mom and my cousin brother:

I am very grateful to my dad, who meticulously edited my manuscript, eliminating repetitive words and sentences, and teaching me the importance of patience throughout the process. His advice to take my time, focus on the content, and present it as neatly as possible was instrumental in shaping this book.

I am deeply grateful to my mom, whose unwavering encouragement kept me inspired to write even during moments of creative drought. Whenever I felt devoid of ideas, she shared stories that ignited the spark in my mind, filling it with vibrant new ideas and possibilities.

I also extend my heartfelt gratitude to my cousin brother, Dhruv Bashetti, who is the same age as of me. His keen eye for detail helped refine my sentences and elevate the vocabulary of the text. His contributions added clarity and richness to the language, significantly enhancing the overall quality of this work.

Their invaluable contributions and unwavering encouragement have been instrumental in bringing this book to life.

Prologue

Introduction

1. Krish: He is 13. His parents died when he was small. The natural leader of the group, Krish is known for his quick thinking and bravery.
2. Ameena: She is 13. She lives in a big mansion with her parents. The most resourceful, Ameena is a skilled herbalist with a deep knowledge of local plants and their properties.
3. Kabir: He is 13. He left his house at the age of 9 to become a warrior. Kabir is known for his physical strength and endurance.
4. Ria: She is 13. Her parents live in a small house, but she lives with Ameena. A talented archer with an uncanny ability to hit her target from great distances. Ria is quiet and reserved but fiercely loyal to her friends and skilled in archery.
5. Amar: He is 10. His parents died in a war when he was small. He is a skilled shooter. He has a lot of knowledge about guns.
6. Sami: She is 12. Her family lives in a mansion, but she like spending time with her friends so she lives with Ameena. The best swimmer, she knows all about the seas, oceans and of course, swimming.

CHAPTER ONE

THE WARRIOR TEENS VS THE CRABA PIRATES

{NARRATOR: Krish}

[Hello, I'm Krish. Me and my friends are gonna narrate this story to you. I hope you'll enjoy it. So, let's start!]

I'll start from the beginning. When I was three years old, I lived with my parents in a small village named Asmynt, it was surrounded by water. The village was terrorized by shark-like creatures named Tarmains. They were five times bigger than a shark. They were light blue in colour and lived in the waters. The Tarmains normally attacked the village one at a time, and mostly the village defended them. But one day, they attacked the village and this time they weren't one or two. There were literally fifty of them. Everyone was shocked and scared. All started running here and there like crazy. My parents quickly took me to the underground chamber. There was an underground chamber where people can hide to save themselves from attacks like these. Then my parents went to save the village. The Tarmains are water-creatures but they have the ability to breathe fire. They burned the whole village to ashes. I waited for them. I could hear the Tarmains and my village people groaning. After all the noises stopped. I came out to see what had happened. When I came up, it was a very bad view. All the people were lying dead. There were just ashes everywhere. One Tarmain was lying dead as well. I saw my parents were floating at the coast of the sea. There were many more people lying dead. The water near them had turned red. I started crying [I think so] By hearing my voice and seeing the red water, some people were attracted. They came to my village and saw me crying, so they took me to an island with them. I grew up there. I made some friends, who are Ameena, Kabir, Ria, Amar and Sami.

10 YEARS LATER-

Till now I was 13 years old. The island I lived on was named Anybo. It was also terrorized by the Tarmains. All the people were scared of the Tarmains. Except us. As the old people of the village say that we are fearless warrior teens. We got this name a few days or months- [Ameena: Exactly 1 month ago.

Ok, now don't disturb me.

Ameena: Sorry.]

Sorry for the disturbance, she was my friend Ameena. So, where was I? Oh, yeah. We got this name a few-I mean exactly 1 month ago. I'll tell you how. We were just hanging out at the beach. When we heard a scream 'Ahh!!! Catch him!' We ran to see what had happened. A thief had stolen someone's jewellery and he was running away. We started running to catch him. You might think we were running to catch him for stealing jewellery. No way! When the thief was running, we saw five packets of *Antigus's Chocolate*. It is a famous brand of chocolate in Anybo and it is really very tasty. So, after running for a few minutes, we were out of the sights of the people. Then we ran faster, because before we were just acting of running. Finally, we caught the thief. I punched him and he fainted. We quickly opened his bag and took out all the chocolates to eat and the jewellery to return back. But with it we also saw a *wanted* poster. Literally! The thief had a bounty of twenty thousand Rs. 20,000! We quickly hid the candy in our pockets and took the thief with us. We went to the village to show them that we had caught him. We returned the jewellery to its owner, everyone started clapping, they also thanked us to catch the thief. Then we went to police station. We handed the thief to the police and, we got twenty thousand rupees! When we came back everyone started calling us the warrior teens. That's how we got this name and till now we have caught many thieves. I don't know the exact number. What was it?

[Kabir: Something around 2-3.

Amar: No, 1-2.

Sami: Nope, 4.

Ria: Stop this nonsense, it's 6.

Everyone, stop fighting!

Ameena: Yeah, Krish's right, stop fighting. The answer is just 2.]

Sorry, my friends always keep fighting. So, we have caught only 2 thieves. I'll skip the part in between; I'll tell directly what happened today.

Do you know pirates? Of course, who doesn't. So, pirates had attacked our island. We didn't even know. We were enjoying Scewla, in the drinks shop at the beach. (Scewla is a type cold drink, it's very delicious.) When we were done, we came out of the drinks shop. We saw the pirates ship was boarded at the coast. We could hear the pirates screaming at the people. Kabir asked "Should we go and attack them?" Ria replied "No, if we attack now. They'll definitely defeat us." Ameena nodded agreement "Yeah, she's right." I said "I have an idea, follow me." I started running. Amar asked "Where are you taking us?" I said "Stop talking and just follow me." Amar started "But just tell us-' "Keep your smelly mouth shut and run faster you sloth!" I interrupted. He nodded angrily. After running for few minutes, we reached our destination-The beach!

Kabir asked "Why did you bring us here?" I replied, pointing at the ship "Because there could be some weapons up there, or something which will help us fight the pirates." Amar said delightfully "Yeah, that's a fantastic idea." There was a rope hanging down the deck. Everyone climbed up behind me as fast as we could. I reached the top. I could see our whole colony from up there. Others came up as well. Most of the things were junk. Like cans of Seriam (A type of liquor in Anybo), packets of food, rusted metal and a lot more. While I was searching in the cabin where the helm is, I saw a wooden barrel with a white cloth on it. I removed the cloth and opened the barrel. When I saw inside, our search had ended. I shouted "Everyone, quickly come here! Quickly! I found it!" Everyone came running and asked while gasping "**gasp** What happened? **gasp** Why are you shouting?" I said "See there are weapons inside this barrel." I showed everyone the barrel. We all were very happy. Everyone took a weapon for themselves. I had taken a claymore sword. Ameena had taken a stick with sharp edges on both sides. Kabir had taken a katana. Ria had taken a bow and arrow. Amar had taken a dart gun. Sami had taken a slingshot.

I took the binoculars and saw what was happening. The pirates were looting everyone's houses. We quickly ran towards our houses.

AT THE COLONY

The pirates were hitting people with back of their swords. We somehow had managed to climb up on the roofs of the houses. We were ready to attack. I looked at Ria and asked "Ready?"

She nodded "Ready." I turned back to the pirates.

She aimed at a pirate who was just about to hit someone. Without taking her eyes off the target, her fingers led the nock to the string, while her arm raised the bow to her cheek. She pulled the bow taut. 5 seconds until the pirate hit the person. She closed her eyes. 4 seconds to go. Took a deep breath. 3 seconds to go. Exhaled. 2 seconds to go. Opened her eyes. 1 second to go. Finally, she let the arrow go. It went straight into the pirate's head. He fell down. All the pirates were now alert. I and Kabir jumped down the roof. All the pirates turned their heads towards us. We were their target. One pirate came running towards me and tried to hit me in the head but I dodged it and stabbed my sword into his stomach. He groaned "Ahh!" I took the sword out and he fell down.

Two pirates came running towards Kabir. He stroked both the pirates in the chest and they fell down. Suddenly, a pirate came running from behind us. We were shocked and were confused what to do. When an arrow came and struck the pirate in the head. The pirate fell down. It was Ria, she killed the pirate. We both said "Thanks" and turned back to the other pirates. We ran towards the pirates. One came with a sharp dagger in his hand. I quickly hit him in the head with the broad side of my sword. I took the dagger from his hand and kept it with me (It can come in handy). Another one came running with a katana in his left hand as well. Kabir dodged his attack and then hit his shoulder. Which made the pirate's katana fall down. The pirate groaned in pain. Then Kabir slashed his sword into the pirate's stomach. The pirate fell down. Kabir took his sword and stood in the fighting position. He said "Now see what I do to you guys." Kabir spread his hands like a bird. Katana in his both hands. He took his right leg forward and bent down a bit. He looked like Zoro. All the pirates came running towards Kabir. He ran with full speed, hitting all the pirates in the stomach. Kabir liked playing with swords. He practiced every day. His all work came in handy now. Almost hitting more than 50 pirates, he stopped. All the pirates fell down. Kabir's both swords were filled with blood.

One pirate, who was tall and looked like their captain said "Ahh! That's enough!" He removed something from his pocket. They were *balls-wooden balls*. He clicked a button which made a sound like ***clink*** and threw it towards us. Before we could do anything, the *balls* exploded. Me and Kabir crashed into the house on our left side. Amar, Ameena and Ria crashed onto the wall on their right. We all fell unconscious...

When I woke up, everything was blur. I could feel that my lip was bleeding. I was tied to a wooden chair on which I was sitting. When my vision got clear. I looked around, all my friends were sitting on a chair beside me with their hands tied as well. All our weapons were thrown at a corner. I knew wherever I was, I was in trouble. So, I had to get out as fast as possible. Then I remembered, that dagger. Which I had taken from the pirate. I saw towards my pocket. The dagger was peeking out of my pocket. I tried to move my hands towards my right pocket a bit. Then I shook my right leg and guess what, the dagger fell out into my hand. I started cutting the rope but it was very hard. I thought I was almost done. When suddenly, a pirate appeared in front of me. He asked in a rough voice "Kiddy, ready to *die*?" He took his sword out of the brown-coloured leather scabbard. His sword was shining a lot and was also very clean. I knew I was gonna die so I just stopped cutting the rope. There was something carved on the blade of his sword. The carving said – "ライフテイカー"

It was in Japanese, but I know Japanese a little bit. It means 'Life Taker' in English. The pirate aimed his sword for my head. The others had already woken up. He counted "***3...2...1...*** *and go!*" The sword was just a few centimetres away from my head. When suddenly, a sharp rock shot into the pirate's head killing him on-the-spot. We were surprised, when we saw towards the direction from where the rock had come, we saw Sami. Sami hadn't come down from the roof yet! I quickly started cutting the rope again and I cut it. I quickly jumped towards our weapons and took my and Kabir's sword. I cut the rope which was tied to Kabir's hands and gave him the katana so he could free the others as well. One pirate came to attack me, I slashed my sword in his chest and he fell down. Suddenly, out of nowhere a pirate came and attacked me on the head. I quickly blocked his attack with my sword. But he was way much stronger than me. My head was just going to get cut when a dart shot into the pirate's neck and he fell unconscious. It was Amar. He shot the pirate. I said "Thank you!" and ran to the other pirates. Only six pirates were remaining. We all gathered together.

Now it was:

The Warrior Teens vs The Craba Pirates

Oh, I forgot to tell the pirates crew name was Craba Pirates. I commanded "Everyone, attack!" We all ran towards the pirates and all the pirates ran towards us. I went towards their boss. He hit many blows together and it was very hard to block them but I manged it. I didn't know what was happening with the others. I could just hear the clash of the swords and groans. I fought with the pirate for a long time. Now both of us were tired. My head was bleeding a little bit. Finally, he took a small 1 second stop to breathe in some air. I knew this was my last chance. I quickly stabbed the sword into his stomach and he groaned loudly "Ahh!" I pulled out the sword which was now filled with blood. The pirate fell down to his knees and then on his face. A second after that, everyone started clapping and cheering "Woohoo! The Warrior Teens saved us! Yay! Woohoo!" We went to the hospital. I bandaged my head. The others had small injuries like scratches or small cuts. When we came out of the hospital, one family asked us to come at their house for dinner, and of course we said yes! Because after fighting the pirates we were very hungry. And you might be thinking what happened to the pirates and their ship. So, we sent the pirates to the police, and about the ship. It is still docked at the beach.

The food was very tasty at their house, we ate literally like dogs, just munching on every food we saw. After dinner we went to our house to sleep. We all sleep at Ameena's house because some of us don't have parents, some left them to follow their dream and some just for fun. It was something around 12:30 A.M. until we slept.

I slept quietly. While I was sleeping, I heard some screams. I thought it might be a dream. But agaïn, I heard someone scream. I opened my eyes. The sun was shining brightly outside. When I saw the sun shining, I was 100% sure it was a dream. But again, I heard a scream. I woke up, woke the others as well and brushed quickly. After we were done, we went outside to see what was going on. There was nothing, everything was normal. It was so peaceful, there was only the sounds of water splashing and the breeze. Suddenly, the ground started rumbling. I heard roar of something and at that second, we knew of what it was.

The *Tarmains*! We ran towards the direction from where the noise was coming. When we reached, we saw a Tarmain was burning all the houses using flames. The Tarmain had attacked near the house where we had kept the Antigus's Chocolates so no one would find it. The weapons we took in yesterday's fight were still with us. So, we quickly took out our weapons. Amar tried shooting a dart at it so it will faint. But the dart didn't work. So, Ria shot an arrow straight into its neck. It groaned loudly. Now, it was alerted and heading for us. We started running away from it. While it slithered towards us its body crushed the hiding place of the chocolate. We all were very angry. Because the chocolates cost literally, Rs. 1000 and it is rarely available in the shops because it's a bestseller. Ria turned around angrily and aimed the arrow towards the Tarmain's eye. She shot it. The Tarmain groaned very loudly. We knew this was our chance or else it would kill us. Ria shot another arrow into its another eye. Me and Kabir quickly ran towards the Tarmain. I quickly jumped as high as I could and reached its chest. I quickly stabbed my sword into its flesh so I wouldn't fall down. There

was a small rope in my pocket. I removed it out and tied one end onto my waist and the other end onto the sword's hilt. Now, I was hanging. Kabir threw both the katanas towards me and I caught it. I stabbed both the katanas into its flesh and pulled it out. The Tarmain was moving so rapidly as it was hurt. I was washed down to the ground with the blood. My sword also got pulled out as I fell down. The Tarmain started falling. I quickly moved out of its way and it crashed down. The wind which was formed by falling of the Tarmain threw me into a house breaking its door.

When I woke up, I was surrounded by many people. I stood up and everyone clapped for us. Guess what, I hadn't even got any big injuries. Just a small cut, we went to Ameena's house where her mother bandaged my head where I had gotten hurt and also made us hot chocolate. Everyone except me and Kabir were laughing and talking about the fight. Sami asked to me and Kabir "Why are you sitting so quiet?" We both unexpectedly replied together angrily "The mad Tarmain destroyed all our Antigus's chocolates! They are so costly and rarely available anywhere!" We both quickly looked at each other. He started "Jin-" But I quickly said before he ended "Jinx!" He thumped his fist on the sofa. I giggled silently. Ria frustrated "When will you stop doing these childish things?" I said "Over." He sighed and said "I'll get you back for this." She said "Stop it." We apologised. There was a long silence, no one said anything. But I broke the silence "That's enough! I'm going to kill all the Tarmains for destroying our chocolates and killing my parents! If anyone wants to come, follow me. No one can stop me from ending their terrorism." Ameena started "But-" I interrupted "No one will stop me. I have made up my mind." I went walking towards the main door acting like I had a plan ready. But my mind was completely empty. Hee-hee. Sami said "It's okay you want to take revenge from them because they killed your parents but chocolates, really!" For a second, I thought no one was gonna come. But then Kabir stood up and said "Roger." I asked "What do you mean?" He said "Oh, come on. You ruined the heroic moment! You said that 'follow me' that's why I said 'roger'! You silly kid." I said "Hey, I'm not a silly kid and sorry and let's go!" He sighed and followed me. Amar stood up and followed us as well. Ria stood up and said "Everyone is going. I've to go as well." We were surprised that Ria was coming as well. So, if Ria was coming the other girls had to come as well. Because she was their best friend.

When we came out of the house, everyone asked "What's the plan?" I stammered "Um...uh...plan, right? Hee...nothing." Everyone screamed "What!" Ria shouted "There's no plan, we left the hot chocolate because of you." 'Sorry, go and drink the hot chocolate, till then I'll make a plan.' 'Okay' 'I will tell you the plan till tomorrow.'

'OK'

I tried making a plan, but I couldn't. The only way to destroy all the Tarmains was to go at the Killer's Pool and attack them. The Killer's Pool is said to be a mythical island where all the Tarmains live. Everyone think it is just a myth, but we-The Warrior Teens think that it is for real. But the other people just don't listen to us. The problem is even if there really is something like the Killer's Pool, how were we gonna get there because we'd have to sail the whole ocean.

I was very tired, so I went to the beach. I thought I might get some ideas because of the calm environment, sounds of the waves, birds chirping and the cool breeze. I took a notebook, a pen and a pencil and went to the beach. It was very calm, no one was there. I sat on the soft sand, watching the sunset in the cool breeze. I was sitting at the beach when I heard a creak. When I saw towards the direction of the noise. Some people were trying to push the pirates ship, which was still docked at the beach. When I saw towards the ship, an amazing idea struck my mind. Actually, the idea's normal, anyone would get it. But my mind wasn't working. I quickly ran towards the people and asked "What are you doing?" They said "What do you mean by that? Can't you see we are pushing the ship into the ocean so no other pirates will come here to attack us." I said "No! Don't do it, I need the ship!" They asked roughly "Who are you, the king or The Warrior Teens? Why should we listen to you?" I replied "I'm the leader of The Warrior Teens." I thought this would stop them, but instead they started laughing and said "Hahaha! Stop acting Kiddy, go home and sleep or else your mom will scold you. Hahahaha!" It showed that they were not from our colony but still this...was very insulting. I shouted "I am the leader of, The Warrior Teens! Ask anyone here!" Hearing me shouting, an old man came to see what happened. He came and looked at me. He was surprised to see me; I could tell it from his expression. He bowed down to me. The other people asked "Hey, old man, why are you bowing down to this little puny?" The old man said with a shocked expression "Abhirda, he is the leader of The Warrior Teens! Show him some respect!" The people looked at me, shocked. They quickly bowed down and said "Please forgive us." I said trying to look super cool "I'm no villain. I've forgiven you already." They said "Thank you." And went away. I wrote my whole idea into the notebook.

By the time I was done, it was something around 11:30 P.M. I quickly went to sleep. When I reached home, the lights were off, the TV was on and everyone was asleep on the sofa. I switched off the TV and went into my room to sleep.

CHAPTER TWO

BATTLE WITH A TIGER!

{NARRATOR: Kabir}

[Ria: Hey! I was waiting for so long! It's my chance now!

Sorry, I took the mic. Hahaha!

Hello! I'm Kabir, Krish's friend and I am gonna narrate this chapter to you. It's my first chapter, I hope you enjoy it.]

When I woke up, the sun was shining brightly. The birds were chirping and I was sleeping on the sofa. The others were asleep as well. I managed to get out of the hall and went to brush my teeth. When I went back into the hall; everyone was sleeping but Krish was awake. I asked him "Have you made a plan?" He replied "Yep." 'Then when will you show it?' 'When everyone will wake up.' 'Oh, ok.'.

Until then, I bathed and got ready. When I came into the hall, everyone was awake and ready as well. They were waiting for me. I went and sat on the sofa. Krish opened his notebook, read something and then said "So, our plan is-

We're gonna go and sail on the pirate's ship which is still docked at the beach. Then, we'll go, attack the Tarmains, we will win the battle and kill all of them!"

Ria said "The start was good, but the mid and the end was like a child's plan." Krish asked "Sorry, but how's it?" Everyone said "Actually, it's good. We should go on with it."

"So, everyone, get ready quickly! We're gonna set sail to the Killer's Pool!" said Krish ending the conversation. We all went to get ready. After a few minutes everyone was ready.

Krish asked to me "Should we go and check the ship?" I replied "Yeah, why not." Krish said to the others "Me and Kabir are going to check the ship." The others said "OK" We went to the beach. It was very calm. No one was there. Krish climbed up first and I went after him. We went to the main cabin. Where the helm is. It was moving smoothly. It was good news but suddenly we heard a crash. We weren't alone on the ship. I asked "What was that?" Krish said "I don't know." 'Is it one of your pranks, Krish? If it is, then just stop it!' 'No way! Do you think I can do such a thing?' 'Yeah.' 'Ok, just stop.' 'OK'

We peeked out of the cabin and what we saw was shocking. There was a Tiger on the ship! I screamed "Ahh!" He snaped "Shut up! You fool! You'll get us both killed." I apologised. We got out of the cabin without making any noise like a thief. There was some space behind the cabin, so we hid there. Krish peeked out form the corner. Then turned towards the wooden barrels kept behind us. He was looking at the barrel which was at the centre. There was ribbon on it, which said: MEAT

He turned towards me and whispered "I have an idea!" I asked "What?!" He went towards the barrel of meat. He opened it and took out a few slices of meat, and gave them to me. He said "When I say 'GO!' throw these towards me." I started "Ok, but-" He ran towards the tiger even before I could complete my sentence.

He shouted "Hey! Tiger, fight me!" I thought in my mind "Is he mad?!" That was enough to get the tiger's attention. He looked at Krish angrily and roared loudly. Krish went running in front of the tiger. He looked down to a big metal chain near his leg. The tiger went running towards Krish. Krish quickly rolled under him, took the chain and tied it around the tiger's neck. He quickly ran towards a wooden pole; he tied the other end to the pole and quickly got out of its way. He said "GO!" to me. I threw the meat towards him and he caught it. Now the tiger was stuck. Krish kept the pieces of meat beside him and sat down on his knees. The tiger roared loudly. Krish shouted loudly "Shut up!!!" and the tiger suddenly went silent. Krish took his left hand forward and kept it on the ground. He said "Listen to me neatly. I'll give you two options. First, we'll free you and then you can go anywhere you want but you won't get any food to eat on this island. And the people living here are hunters." He took his right hand forward and kept it down and said "Option two, you'll have to stay with us and we will not tie you but only if you won't attack anyone from our team. And if you stay with us, I'll also give you this meat every day."

The tiger looked at Krish's left hand and then his right hand.

I started laughing and said "Hahaha...how will it answer? It won't answer. Hahaha!"

Surprisingly, the tiger took its left hand forward and kept it on Krish's right hand! Which meant he chose option two! Really!? Wow! Krish continued "But you have to promise that you won't eat anyone from our team. OK?" The tiger nodded. It looked like it was understanding everything what Krish was saying. Krish commanded to the tiger "Just stay here tiger and don't run away. We're going to call our team." The tiger roared loudly. I asked Krish "What happened?" Krish replied "I know, he doesn't like us calling him tiger. We should give him a name. Do you want a name?" The tiger nodded. I don't know how but Krish was right. The tiger nodded. I suggested "Killer." Krish shouted "No! He's not violent or any killer. Hey, how's this. Chikimuku?" Before I could even open my mouth, he continued "Yeah, that's good! Do you like it Chikimuku?" The tiger-I mean Chi-ki-muku nodded. Krish said "So, Chikimuku is your name. Okay, Chikimuku, now just stay here and don't run away. We're going to call our team." Chikimuku nodded and sat down quietly like a good boy.

When we reached, everyone was ready. We opened the door and then Ameena said something which delayed us a lot. She said "Bye, mom!" Her mom quickly came and asked "Where are you going?" I was gonna tell Ameena to tell her mom that we were just going for a ride. But she happily told the truth! "We are going to the Killer's Pool to end all the Tarmains!" Her mom said with shock "What?! How dare you?! No way! You're not going! Are you mad?! And there's no such thing as 'The Killer's Pool'!" Ameena said "It is there."

The World War 3 had started. Hahaha! So, to stop it, Amar interrupted "Please Aunt, let her come. We promise she'll not get hurt." I thought her mom wouldn't agree but surprisingly she said "Are you sure?" Sami quickly answered "Yes, we promise!" 'OK, go.' 'Thank You!' We started our walk to the ship. While walking I got an idea to scare everyone, I called Krish to a corner and told him the whole plan.

He laughed and said "It's a good idea." I said to the others "Me and Krish forgot to bring something. We're going to bring it. So, till then go to the ship and wait for us. Okay?" Ria said "OK." We acted like we were going towards Ameena's house. But when we got out of their sight, we quickly took a shortcut to the beach, so we could reach the ship before they could.

In a minute we were at the beach. We quickly climbed up. When we reached the deck, I saw them. The others had almost reached the beach. I quickly called out to Krish "Krish! The others have reached! Do *it* quickly!" He replied "Yes! Almost done."

Krish came running and said "Done!" I commanded "Okay, so let's hide now." 'Oh, yeah. I forgot. But where should we hide?' 'Um...I don't know. I thought you might know a good place.' 'Idea! The cabin!' 'Oh, that's a good idea! They can even hear the voice neatly.' 'Yeah, let's go! They are almost here.'

We quickly hid in the cabin with Chikimuku, a...a tiger!

We peeked through the door. The others had climbed up the ship and were waiting for us. At that time, I quickly opened the door, making enough space for Chikimuku to go through. He roared loudly, which attracted everyone. Everyone got scared. Krish said trying to make his voice sound like an adult or tiger "I am Chikimuku, the ghost of the owner of this ship. Hahahaha! Now, I'm gonna eat you." Chikimuku understands what we say, so Krish had told him the plan and what to do, and when to do. So, Chikimuku started walking towards the others. Everyone started screaming "Help us! We don't want to die! Nooooooooooooo!" Everyone closed their eyes like they knew this was their end. When Chikimuku was just a few centimetres away from them. We thud open the door and came out laughing "Hahahahaha! It was great fun making a fool of you! Hahahaha!" All of them shouted loudly "It was you! Then, who is this t...tiger?! How was it talking?! What exactly happened?!

We explained them everything. But we shouldn't have. Because after that they hit a us like dog. It was very bad.

We were getting ready to start our journey to the Killer's Pool.

Ria said "Krish, this name is pretty bad, Chi-ki-muku. It's so hard to pronounce." Krish said "Yeah, I know. Bit still, it's good. Hee-hee."

Krish did all the arrangements like taking up the anchor, raising the flag and the sail. Now we were 100% ready to start our journey! Krish went in the cabin, kept his hands on the helm and asked loudly "Should we go?!" We all shouted together "Let's Go!!!"

And then Krish moved the helm and the ship started moving neatly! Our journey had finally started. Now, who knows what will be waiting for us. But I know that there are gonna be a lot of adventures on the line!

CHAPTER THREE

THE OUT-OF-THE WORLD PORTAL!

{NARRATOR: Ria}

[Hey! Amar, give me back the mic!

Amar: Nope! Hee-hee...

Come here!

Amar: Ouch! Why did you hit me so hard?!

You know the reason. Give me the mic! Ooh...finally, I got the mic. Now, I can narrate this chapter. I'm very excited, it's my first time narrating a chapter like this! Yes! Let's go!]

So, finally our journey to the Killer's Pool has started. I don't know how much time it will take but I know it will take a lot of time. What am I saying? Even I don't know. Haha! Oh, sorry I'm going off the main topic. I'll tell you what happened in our journey. And if you're wondering where is Chikimuku. So, he's safe, enjoying in the cargo hold.

Sami asked Krish "So, where is the map?" Krish said "Map? Which map? I don't have any map." She shouted "What do you mean by you don't have a map?! How are we gonna go to the Killer's Pool without a map?!" Krish said calmly "Oh, yeah. You're right." She shouted again "You realized it just now!" Sami's a bit short-tempered, so she gets a little bit angry-okay, a lot angry sometimes. Ameena said "So, our next task is to find a map! Woohoo!" I asked "How or where are we gonna find a map?" The second I said it we heard a loud ***boom***. We saw towards the direction form where the sound had come. There were two ships. One was of pirates and the other one was of the navy. There was a battle going on between them. The pirate ship had attacked the navy ship. The navy ship was destroyed a lot. The pirate ship was continuously attacking the navy ship. Finally, after a few minutes, the navy ship blasted and sank to the bottom. While the pirate ship was turning around it saw us and its motor went off. Then after a few seconds the motor started, and now they were coming for us. Ameena shouted to Krish "Krish! Let's get away from here!" He said "Aye-Aye!" and went into the cabin. The propeller started and we got a little far from them. After some time, I thought we had lost their tail. But that second a bullet shot logs of wood which were tied using a rope. All the logs were now rolling here and there freely. The logs of wood were making everyone fall. A log came rolling towards my legs and I jumped up dodging it. But when I came down two more logs came rolling. I managed to dodge one but the second one made me fall. Another bullet shot into a lantern which was hanged to a wooden pillar which was of the main mast. One more bullet shot into the cabin breaking its glass, where Krish was. A piece of the broken glass flew in air and hit into Krish's cheek. His cheek was bleeding. That disturbed him and he lost control. The ship started shaking, going up and down. We all were crashing from here to there. On the corner there was a barrel. It fell and some liquid started leaking through it. We didn't know what it was but it looked like Krish knew. Because there was tension visible on his face. He quickly opened the cabin's door and came running. Krish saw towards the pirate ship. Then looked back to the leaking barrel. He lifted up the barrel and waited for some time. The pirate ship was closing in. Now the pirate ship was so close we could even see the men holding guns, their fingers near the trigger. One man was almost gonna shoot at him. At the last second, Krish threw the leaking barrel towards the man and exactly he shot at that time. Krish quickly bent down getting cover. The bullet hit the barrel and it exploded. The pirate ship was fully on fire. We all stood up and looked at the ship. We thought the men had just fainted but they were dead. Kabir said to Krish "Krish, let's get out of here! Before any more pirates come." Krish was going towards the cabin but suddenly he stopped. He looked back towards the ship and went running towards it. He jumped high and landed into the burning pirate ship. Amar shouted to Krish "Hey Krish! Are you mad?!What the heck are you doing?!" He opened a small drawer in the ship. Something like paper roll was peeking out of it. He took it out and kept it in his pocket. Then he grabbed the gun which was fallen near his leg and jumped back.

Sami asked "What's that?" Krish unrolled the paper and said showing it to us "A map."

I asked Krish "Good job about the gun but how did you know there's a map there as well?" He replied "I just thought that there can be a map because they are pirates, they sail to many places." Kabir said "Oh, yeah. That's right."

Ameena said looking at the burning pirate boat "We shouldn't have ***killed*** them. If the other pirates find out about this, it's gonna be a very bad news for us." Amar said without any tension "Oh, come on. They won't be able to find it. Until they come the ship will be drowned deep under the water

An hour passed by after the pirate ship event. No one could understand where we were on the map. So, no one was using it and the map was just rolling from here to there on the wood. We all were busy looking at the gun and examining it. I asked "Which gun is this?" Amar replied "It's a *gold-plated Colt 45 Revolver! It was invented by Charles Brinckerhoff Richards and William Mason in the year 1873*" He knows a lot about guns. Really! It was a ***gold-plated Colt 45 Revolver***! While we were examining the gun, we heard a loud lightning struck. When we saw up the sky was fully grey. The climate suddenly had changed to gloomy and dark. We could see and hear a lot of lightning struck. The waves started to rise up and up. Krish commanded to Sami "Sami, check the map! Where are we?!" She went running towards the map and started finding where we were. She looked at us in shock and said "Everyone quickly come here!" We all went running towards her. Ameena asked "What happened? Where are we?" She replied "We...are...in-" "Don't create suspense! Tell us quickly!" Amar snapped. She continued "We are in the Teiosaan Sea!" No one was shocked at all. No one even moved. Amar asked "What's that?" She shouted "What?! You idiot! Don't you know what that is?!" We all said together "We don't know as well. What's that?" She said "Oh! It' one of the most dangerous seas! It has killed many people." Krish asked with a life-less expression on his face "Should we be worried about it?" She shouted "Yes! Of course!!!" Kabir said "Oh, ok...ok. Just calm down." 'Ooh, we should get away from here now.' The second she said it, the ship started going up and down. Large waves started crashing on our ship.

A big wave came and crashed onto the deck and I fell on my face. The thunderstorm was rising rapidly, the waves were rising higher than our ship's length. Another big wave came which was a lot bigger than our ship's length. Krish went running towards the hatch and opened it. He commanded "Everyone, get in! Quick! Be quick! The wave's coming!" We all went running towards the hatch. We all climbed down into the cargo hold where Chikimuku was.

The second Krish closed the hatch we heard a very, very loud thud. It was the sound of the wave crashing onto our ship. For a second everything stopped moving. We thought the thunderstorm had ended. But then we heard another wave crashing onto our ship. It's sound was ten times louder than the before one. Our ship started shaking violently. Our ship started rotating. I went up and down, up and again down. I started feeling *dizzy*. My eyelids started feeling heavy. I closed my eyes and soon I went unconscious.

When I woke up, I was fallen on a big wooden crate in the cargo hold. The others were unconscious. I managed to stand up and then stretched up a bit. It was pretty quiet. It looked like the storm had finally ended. I woke everyone up and then we went up onto the deck to check what was happening. The storm had ended. The sun had rose. The water was clam. The weather was calm. There was a cool breeze. We were hungry, the food we had brought with us was destroyed because of the thunderstorm. Krish said "We should search for an island or village. We can get some food there." Sami said "Oh, yeah. That's a good idea. Wait, I'll check if any island is there on our way, on the map." She went and searched. We were also keeping an eye, if we see any island. There was nothing except the water. Sami said excitedly "Yes! There's an island on our way. It's straight ahead." She looked at a few rocks which were floating on the water, then looked back into the map. Then looked towards us and said "It's something around 6-9 kilometres away. We'll reach there in a few minutes." Krish went in the cabin and our ship was sailing faster than before.

After ten minutes we could saw an island. Ameena said pointing at the island "See! We're here." Krish smoothly docked the ship at a beach on the island. We climbed down the ship. Krish asked to Sami "What's the island's name?" Sami had kept the map into her pocket. So, she took it out, unrolled it and said "Ecuivoc Island." "Hmm...weird name." Krish said ending the conversation. The island was full of trees. There were no living organisms. There was no sign of food. We searched here and there for minutes. We finally stopped. Because of no food, our energy had drained out. We thought to give it a final try and started the food finding operation again. But still we found nothing. We were searching everywhere, when suddenly Amar shouted "Help! Help!" We all went near him to see what happened. There was quick sand and he was getting sucked in. We all grabbed both of his hands and started pulling him with our last bits of energy. But instead of taking him out we all fell in as well. When I got in. I started feeling that my body was getting crushed from all sides. I closed my eyes because of the unbearable pain. I was losing my breath as well.

Suddenly, all the pain and crushing stopped. My breath returned. I took a deep breath, opened my eyes and exhaled the air. I was lying on soft sand. I stood up. The others stood up as well. We were somewhere else. The sand was very, very soft. The sky was purple. We were surrounded by cute flowers and bright plants. There was a sweet scent. We heard a sound like '***swish***'. I turned back. There was a lot of light which blinded me partially for a second. The light fainted and what we saw was breath-taking. There was a big **Portal**...!! On the other side of the portal; the Sun was rising, there was a very bright farm. I don't know how but suddenly I was getting attracted towards it. My body started moving by itself. It was happening the same with the others. Now the portal was just a few centimetres away from us. We could see a lot of things from it. We all looked at each and nodded. I took a deep breath and exhaled it. Everyone said together "***3...2...1... and go!!!***" *We all jumped into the Portal.* The next view I saw was amazing, breath-taking, over-whelming and whatever there is!

CHAPTER FOUR

"WHOSE HARBOUSIS DRINKING CEREMONY, IS IT?"

{NARRATOR: Amar}

[Hee-hee! Hello! I'm Amar! I'm gonna narrate this chapter, I hope you like it. Hee-hee! And-

Kabir: Don't waste the reader's time. Start the chapter.

Ok, I'll start now.]

We jumped into the- [Ria: Hey, that's done. I said that. Narrate the next part.] OK. The view was amazing! We were in a new world! We were surrounded by a big and bright farm. The sun had just rose. The portal behind us suddenly closed. Now we were stuck in a different world. So, we started exploring the farm. While exploring I found a unique fruit hanging to a tree. I pulled it down. But instead of being a fruit, it was a honey bee! It started chasing me. Later, others noticed the bee and the bee noticed the others. Hee-hee. It was also chasing the others. After a long chase we thought it lost our tail. I let a sigh of relief when suddenly it appeared out of nowhere and stung Krish on his left hand. A line of blood started dripping down his hand. Krish fell down. The sting's venom was rapidly taking over his body. His arm was turning green. We all went running towards him. The bee's next target was Ria. It was rapidly going towards her. When suddenly an arrow shot into the bee. The bee and arrow fell down. A few unknown people came with bow and arrow in their hands. The people took out an arrow from there quivers and aimed towards us. One of them said "Dauke su! Ba su duba daga nan. Kame su!" Another one said "Lafiya Ubangiji. Zan yi. Mutanen kauye sun kama su!" All the other men said "Lafiya kyaftin!" The other men started coming near us, with their arrows aimed for our heads. When Ria shouted "No, please don't kill us. We need help. We are not enemy." The man said "Tsaya Kada ku kashe su." The others said "Lafiya kyaftin" and lowered their bow and arrows. Ria continued "Thanks, but sorry we aren't getting what you're saying. We need help, he is hurt." The man tried to say in English "F-f-ollo-w mi." It was hard but we understood it. It meant 'Follow me' We followed them. We walked for a lot of hours.

Finally, we reached our destination-I mean their destination. It was a village in a dense but bright jungle. Many people were living there. Some of the people took Krish to some type of hospital and we followed them. We reached it. They kept Krish on a bed made up of leaves and other spongy materials. It was made up of leaves but still looked very cozy and comfortable. Half of the people working there went out and brought some leaves. One lady took the leaves and crushed them into a paste. Then she added some more things into it and mixed it as well. Then she added some spices and water. After a few seconds it was ready, she took the paste and applied where the bee had stung Krish. He started groaning loudly and suddenly started snoring. Weird. One man tried to say "Hii w-will get well in a few m-minute-s." I said "OK."

We waited for him to wake up and in just five minutes he woke up. We said "Thank You." Krish asked "Can we get some food?" Because of the bee chase and the portal thing, we forgot about our hunger. But when Krish said the word '*food*', the hunger came back running. They said "Es. W-why not." I guess they meant 'Yes. Why not.' Because after that they gave us a big feast. We ate everything in a minute. After eating, our stomachs were full.

The main, tall man took us back to the centre of the village and said to the villagers "Kowa, yi Harbousis. Za mu yi bikin shan Harbousis bayan shekaru!" All the people started screaming, celebrating, cheering or shouting [I don't know what were they doing] "Ee! Woohoo! Za mu yi bikin shan Harbousis!"

They all were talking about something called Harbousis. [Am I right?

Krish: No! You made the readers sad!

Oh, I'm sorry.

Ameena: Yes, you are right!

What?

Krish: Hahaha! I was just joking! Hahaha!

You!!!

Krish: Ouch! Ouch! Sorry! Sorry! I'm sorry!

Ok-ok. Don't do it again.

Krish: Okay, hee-hee!

Again?

Krish: Ouch!!!]

Then, they called a man who knew English. I guess he was their translator. The main man said something to the translator man. And the man said "Hello!" We all introduced ourselves. I asked "Which language are the others talking in?" He said "They are talking in Peltickhan. It's the language spoken here." Krish asked "Where do you mean by 'here'? Where are we?" The translator man replied "You are in Peltica"

'What is Peltica?' 'Peltica is a sacred and ancient island.' 'OK, but why is its entry through a jungle on an isolated island?' 'Because we don't want other harmful people to destroy this island. I'm surprised how the Kabedo Mi Portal let you enter in.' 'What's that?' 'It's the portal through which you entered. It doesn't let anyone enter. Only who have a good intention and pure heart, can also rarely enter. The others get burned or shocked with electricity.' 'OK and what were the others saying something like 'Harbousis'. And what's the main, tall man's name? I have a lot of questions coming. Tell us quickly.' 'Ok, ok. Slow down. Harbousis is a drink; after drinking it you'll be able to hear everything in English and not in Peltickhan. The tall man is the village's safety head and his name is Tsaro Shugaban.' 'Ok, and-' 'Stop! Just stop. I'll tell you everything in detail later on. Now come on. It's time for the Harbousis Drinking Ceremony.' 'Only one last question I forgot to ask. Please can I ask?' 'Ok, go on.' 'What's your name?' 'Oh, I am Fassara Sarki.'

Kabir asked "Whose Harbousis Drinking Ceremony, is it?" Fassara replied "Of course, it's yours!" "Oh, ok." Kabir said ending the conversation.

There was a big stage with a red carpet applied on it. It was surrounded by a very large crowd. It looked like there were people not only from the village but also from the outside as well. There were many lightings surrounding the stage. It looked like it was a festival! There was a golden throne kept on the stage. Which I guess, was for us. One old man stepped up on the stage. The old man had a long white beard which went below his neck, he had dark brown eyes. He wore a white coloured woollen shirt and a long red coloured cloak which almost went below his feet. He also wore circular shaped specs. Ria asked "Who's that?" Fassara replied "He's Dumbbus Abelerd, the village's head."

'OH'

Everyone was shouting a lot; their faces were full of excitement and joy. Mr. Abelerd started searching his cloak's pocket for something. He took something out. It was a candy! There was something written on its wrapper. And it was in English! It said:

Loud Voice

He unwrapped it. The candy was of navy-blue colour. Mr. Abelerd kept it in his mouth. He started chewing it. 5 seconds later he gulped it down. He took out another candy, which's wrapper said:

Translate

He unwrapped the second chocolate as well. It was in orange colour. Mr. Abelerd ate it and spoke in English in a very loud voice "Everyone, stay quiet and calm!" I understood why it was written 'Loud Voice' and 'Translate' on its wrapper.

His voice was loud, but kind and humble as well and not at all rough, even being 69 years old (Fassara told us that he was 69 years old). Mr. Abelerd continued "Thank you for staying quiet. I order to bring the Harbousis on the stage."

Two big and fat men came walking slowly with a very-very big transparent pot on their shoulders. The pot was filled with some red coloured liquid which looked like blood. I asked Fassara "What's that?" He replied "That... is the great...-' Sami snapped "Don't make it cinematic." "Oh, sorry. Hee-hee. It is the Harbousis." Said Fassara. 'Oh.'

Smoke was coming through the pot. It looked pretty much hot. The fat men stopped. Mr. Abelerd said "I request Amar, Sami, Ria, Kabir, Ameena and Krish to come on the stage."

There were no stairs to climb up so we had to jump up. Mr. Abelerd continued "Amar, please sit on this throne." I followed his command and sat down. Mr. Abelerd told me to open my mouth and I opened it. I was scared a bit. [Ria: Really? A bit? Are you sure?

Ok, I admit I was scared a lot.

Ria: Yeah, that's good!]

Where was I? Yeah! I was scared because the Harbousis looked hot. Smoke was coming through it. Mr. Abelerd commanded the fat men "Pour the Harbousis." The men nodded and lifted the pot. They slowly started turning the pot. My heartbeats fastened. The Harbousis was just a few metres away from my mouth. I closed my eyes and the Harbousis fell into my mouth.

The Harbousis wasn't *hot* at all! It was normal. It tasted like *Coke*! But the next second after drinking it, my eyelids started feeling heavy. My eyes started to close. I tried to keep them open. But I failed and my eyes closed and I fell asleep. In 1-2 minutes, I woke up [Ameena told me I fell asleep. I thought that I just blinked.] and when I woke up, I was able to hear everything in English and not in Peltickhan. I stood up and wiped the drops of Harbousis which were remaining on my mouth by a white handkerchief. I jumped down the stage. After me, it was Sami's turn. She went and sat on the chair. The men poured the Harbousis into her mouth and the same what Ameena told me happened with Sami as well. She slept for a minute or two and woke up. After a few minutes, we all were done.

It was just 12:45 P.M. by now. Mr. Abelerd took Fassara, Tsaro and us to his house for lunch. We reached his house. It was very big. It was almost like a mansion. It was white in colour. Mr. Abelerd's wife-Mrs. Abelerd had made butter chicken for lunch. Which is our-The Warrior Teens favourite dish. We all enjoyed it. After lunch, we washed our hands and sat on the sofa in the living room. Mr Abelerd asked Krish "So, how you came here? What made you come near this island?" Krish explained everything in detail to Mr. Abelerd. "And that's how we reached here." Said Krish ending the big explanation. Mr. Abelerd said "Oh, wow. It's good."

Suddenly, we heard a loud boom. People started screaming. Mr. Abelerd, Tsaro and Fassara's face got tense. Ameena asked "What was that?" Tsaro replied "I think so it's the Rambians!" "What's the Rambians?" asked Sami. Tsaro replied "Rambia is an island which shares its borders with Peltica. The people who live there are called 'Rambians'. The Rambians attack us weekly. They want to capture Peltica. Basically, there's a war going on." Sami continued "So, are they giants?" 'No' 'Then why the ground started shaking?' 'Because they have amazing weapons like bombs, guns and a big army.' 'Oh.'

Tsaro commanded "Fassara, take them and go in cover! Abelerd Sir, let's go!" Mr. Abelerd nodded and went somewhere with Tsaro.

Fassara commanded to us "Guys, quickly follow me! We have to get in cover!" Krish asked "What do you mean by get in cover!? Aren't we gonna fight!?" He replied "Yes, we're going to fight, but not you." 'Why?' 'Because, you're kids!' 'I admit we're kids, but we are not normal. We are brave. Everyone on our island call us 'The Warrior Teens'! We can fight! We have fought!'

Fassara sighed and said "Hmm, okay... come on." We all shouted "Yay!!! Woohoo! Let's go!"

We all followed Fassara. Fassara suddenly stopped and we all crashed into him. I asked "What happened?" He replied "The Rambians." We all looked forward. There stood 10 men with a thin but muscular body. They were having many weapons like axe, katana and etc in their hands. One of them suddenly threw an axe towards us. We quickly ducked down and it hit the wall behind us. We quickly ran away. 5 Rambians started following us. While running I spotted a bomb! Yes, a real bomb! It was a black 'flaming bomb'. I stopped, picked it up and started running again. I asked "Does anyone have a match stick or something?" Fassara replied "Yes, I do. But why do you need it now?" I continued "Just give it quickly!" There was a matchbox hung to his belt, he removed it and gave it to me. I took out one matchstick. It was pretty hard to start the flame as we were running. But finally, I manged to get a small spark and quickly lit the bomb. I turned towards the Rambians and threw the bomb and again hung the matchbox to Fassara's belt. I turned back and ***boom!*** It blasted.

By that loud sound we fell down to our knees. My ears went numb and deaf. My ears were ringing. I couldn't hear anything. By looking at the others expressions their conditions looked the same as well. After a few seconds, I was able to feel my ears and hear everything neatly. We turned back to look if any Rambians were coming for us.

All the Rambians were fallen dead. The ground had turned black and the walls of the houses were completely destroyed. There was fire everywhere. We could hear more Rambians shouting 'Go! Attack! Find the children!' And by the word 'children', they meant us-The Warrior Teens.

We stood up and followed Fassara who led us to a big, clean and white coloured building. It looked like the type of buildings spy agencies use it for their headquarters. Fassara said "This is the PADHO Headquarters." I was right! Headquarters!

Ria asked "Padho? Hmm, what's that?" Fassara continued "It's a short form. The full form is '*Peltica's Attack and Defence Handling Organisation*'. As you can understand from its name. It handles all attack and defence matters of Peltica."

'OH, wow.'

Fassara took out a navy-blue coloured card out of his jeans pocket. On the right side of the card was a passport size photo of Fassara and below it was his age-which was 29. On the left side was his name and what was his work in PADHO-which was a Translator. He swiped the card at the entrance door. And the door opened! By looking at the houses and the way people live there. It looks like they are living in the 60's but actually the technology is pretty advanced. We walked in through the door. The building was bigger inside than it looked from the outside. Many people were there getting ready for the war. Mr. Abelerd and Tsaro were there as well. We quickly ran towards them and told them that the Rambians have already entered Peltica. They are destroying everything. By listening to this, everyone started doing their work faster.

Everyone was *ready* in a few minutes. Tsaro commanded "Krish, Ameena, Kabir, Ria, Amar and Sami you'll stay here. It's safe here. And Fassara you'll come with us." Krish opposed "No way! We don't wanna stay here and wait. We'll battle as well. We are brave! We can fight! We have fought!" Krish copy pasted the same dialogue again. Tsaro started "Bu-" "Tsaro, Krish said the same things to me. First, I didn't listen to them. But later while coming here they fought well. Let them come." Fassara interrupted. One second. Firstly, it isn't "*WE*" it should be "*AMAR*" means me. And second, no one fought. I just threw a bomb towards them which was fallen down on the ground.

Mr. Abelerd asked "Fassara, think again. Are you sure?" "Yes, ***100%***" replied Fassara. Mr. Abelerd continued "Okay, children, you can come." Tsaro turned towards Mr. Abelerd and asked with a frown on his face "Really, sir? Should we?" Mr. Abelerd nodded. Tsaro turned back towards us, sighed and said "Okay, follow me." We followed Tsaro as he said to.

Tsaro took us to the farm where we landed through the-. What was its name? [Ameena: It was something like '***Kabhi do me***'.

Kabir: Yeah! It was...Oh, shoot! I forgot again.

Krish: It is so easy. It's '***Kabedo Mi Portal***'

Oh, yeah. Thanks, Krish.

Krish: Your welcome, Amar.]

So, yeah. *Tsaro* took us to the *farm* where we *landed* through the ***Kabedo Mi Portal***. There was a big army of the *Rambians*. And they looked pretty **fierce** as well.

Ria said "Tsaro, few of the Rambians managed to enter the colony as well. What about them?" Tsaro replied "I've sent a few people there as well to **safeguard** our colony." Ria said ending the conversation "Oh, okay."

The tallest man in their army commanded (or you can say shouted as well because it was very loud) "Rambians, attack!!!"

All the Rambians came running towards us. Tsaro commanded "Everyone, kill them!" We ran towards them as well.

Who is gonna win, who is gonna lose we don't know anything about that. But one thing is sure. Upcoming is a very dangerous ***war***!

CHAPTER FIVE

I AM HATSARI, THE BOSS

{NARRATOR: Krish}

[So, hello guys! I'm back! The ultimate Kri-

Sami: Shut up.

Hey!

Sami: Shut up and start quickly.

Shut up and start quickly! *{He is saying that in a squeaky voice. He is trying to make fun of her. Basically, mimicking her. And who am I? I'm Aarav, the author of this book.}*

Sami: You!!!

Ouch! Ouch! Oh, sorry! Ouch!]

So, the Rambians came running towards us and we went running towards them. The *war* had started. Everyone was hitting each other. We didn't have any weapons so we just had stay quiet in a corner.

But Kabir got an idea! He quickly ran towards a Rambian who was fallen dead. He quickly snatched all his weapons, armour, etc. He came running towards us and put everything on the ground. Everyone took a weapon for themselves. And, sadly no weapons were remaining for me to take.

The armour was just too big and heavy for our bodies. So, we just left it there only. Everyone ran away to fight. But I couldn't, as I didn't have any weapons. While I was looking at the others fight, I spotted a bamboo stick which was anchored in the long grass. I started walking towards the bamboo stick. Suddenly, one man appeared on the other side of the bamboo stick. He definitely was a Rambian. And he wanted the bamboo stick as well. The bamboo stick was in between of us. He came running towards me and punched me on the left side of my face with his right hand. It was pretty hard. I punched him in his stomach with my right hand. He fell down on his knees. I quickly grabbed his head and hit it on the ground two times and then he just didn't stand up again. I quickly ran towards the bamboo stick and held it in my right hand. But out of nowhere, a Rambian came running towards me with a sickle in his left hand. I ducked down, but forgot to take the stick down with me. He cut the bamboo stick in half. I quickly stood up and hit him in the centre of his back with the half-broken bamboo stick in my hand. He screamed loudly "Ahh!!!" and just didn't move. I guess he got paralysed and fell down. I took the second part of the broken stick.

Kabir was fighting one man. And another one was coming from his back to hit him. I quickly throwed the second part of the broken stick towards the man and it hit him in the head. A little bit of *blood* sprinkled out of his head. Kabir shocked, looked towards his back, towards me and then again towards the Rambian. Kabir kicked the Rambian in his stomach and he flew in air and crashed into a tree, breaking it. Kabir turned towards me. He nodded and said "Thanks" I nodded and said "Welcome." He then went running to attack another Rambian. Suddenly, a black flaming ball came flying and crashed in front of me. It took a second for me to understand what it was. It was a *live bomb!* I quickly started running away from it, but even before I get a metre away from it. It blasted! I flew in high in air and crashed onto the ground. Blowing a lot of dust. I guess I wasn't the only one who was affected by the bomb. The Rambians had thrown bombs on the others as well. There was a line of blood on the back of my ear. Which was dripping down towards my shirt. I tried to stand straight but I fell down to my knees. My left hand was paining very much. All the Rambians gathered in front of us in a straight-line side by side. The tallest and fattest one took out a sword from his scabbard. I started regretting my decision of fighting the Rambians. Because I was gonna die without even completing my mission to destroy the Tarmains. It had gotten evening. The sun was at the *horizon.* But still the moon had started to appear. The Rambian aimed the sword for my head. He was gonna hit my head, but suddenly another man shouted "Sir, stop! The moon is here! We have to stop!" He stopped at the position he was. He turned his neck towards the moon and said "Shit! You escaped today, but tomorrow I'm gonna kill you." He put his sword back into the scabbard and then turned back. He commanded "Guys, retreat!" The other Rambians turned back as well and started walking away. Kabir, who was also fallen on his knees asked "You look a pretty dangerous man. What's your name?" The main Rambian replied "Hmm...brave. You have the gut to ask me a question.

I'll answer. I am Hatsari, the boss." He turned back and went away walking.

We all got up and walked back towards the HQ. No one was able to walk neatly. Everyone was *hurt*.

We reached the HQ. Everyone was bandaging their wounds and cuts. I asked Mr. Abelerd "Mr. Abelerd, I didn't understand what were they saying about the moon. Why did he suddenly stopped from killing me?" Mr. Abelerd replied "There is *myth*. That if anyone attacks anyone or battle's when the moon is visible, they'll get a curse. The world's worst curst. It's very gross and danger." I asked curiously "What's the curse?" He replied "Oh, I cannot tell you. You'll need to get an adult to know about it." 'Why?' 'Because it's just too violent. Not at all for your age.' 'Oh, okay.'

I'll skip all the bandaging part, because I don't want to make it *emotional*.

It was something around 10:09 P.M. We were done eating our food. Everyone was sad because we lost the battle and even got badly hurt. One man from our army said "I think so we should just..." Mr. Abelerd asked "What?" He continued "Just...surrender." Tsaro shouted on him "Fool! Are you mad!? Do you know what the heck you said!? Surrender!? No way! We should fight for our land! Our ancestors have fought so hard and brutal wars just for Peltica. And you say we should surrender." Mr. Abelerd said "Calm down, Tsaro." The man apologised "Sorry, sir. I shouldn't have said that." Tsaro calmed down by listening this. The man continued "Now my blood is boiling! Let's kill those $#%&!" Everyone shouted "Yeah!"

We all slept quietly.

THE NEXT DAY

We woke up early at 5:00 A.M. to get ready for the war. Sami asked Tsaro and Mr. Abelerd "How are we gonna defeat them? You said we don't have enough high-tech weapons like them." Tsaro replied "Yeah, you're right. If someone gives us a few weapons I'll literally give them anything." When he said that, I got an amazing idea. I told Kabir, Ria, Amar, Sami and Ameena to gather up. I told them my idea. And they like it! I turned towards Tsaro and said "Ok, Tsaro, listen to me neatly. I have an offer for you. If I-" Suddenly, Ameena kept her hand on my mouth so I couldn't talk. She said in my ear "Krish, I think we should first check if there are any weapons on our ship before making a deal." I thought for a second and replied "Hmm...you're right." I said to Tsaro "Tsaro, we want to go back through the Kabedo Mi Portal. Can you lead us to it?" He replied "Uh, yes. But why?" I replied "You'll know it soon." He sighed and said ending the conversation "Ok, follow me." So, you might have understood what is the plan by now as

Ameena said 'check if there are weapons.'. But I will not tell you the plan. Just watch [or, it will be better to say 'read'] Tsaro led us to the portal and we jumped in. Fassara came with us as well for our safety. We reached the purple sky place. And again, went through the quicksand. Everything happened when we came through the quicksand the first time.

Fassara also had a torch so, we told him to stay near the quicksand so it will be easy for us to find it again. He turned on the torch and turned it towards sky. We quickly ran towards our ship, which visible from the centre of the island. We all climbed up *one-by-one*. I shouted "Let the Operation: Weapon Find began!" Everyone shouted "Yes, let's go!" And the Operation: Weapon Find began. We searched every corner of the ship, but sadly we didn't find any weapons. We were gonna give up, but at the last second, I remembered that we didn't check the cargo hold. Our hope came back. I opened the hatch. And I climbed down the stairs. It was dark in there. I went towards the switches and turned om the lights.

Suddenly, a tiger jumped on me and I fell down. I was full of fear. I was thinking how did a tiger enter our ship. The I remembered that it was Chikimuku, our pet tiger. I calmed down and let a sigh. But he was very angry. And I knew why was he angry. Because we haven't fed him any food in last few days. I said to Chikimuku "Sorry, I'm very sorry, Chikimuku. I know you're hungry. I'll feed you, okay, stop." He didn't He didn't move. I continued "Okay, I'll give you two pieces of meat." No response. "Three pieces." He nodded and let me go. I stood up and said "Guys, wait a minute I'll be back." I quickly ran towards the back of the cabin, where the wooden barrel of meat was kept. I took out three pieces of meat from the wooden barrel. Quickly climbed down the stairs and kept the meat in front of Chikimuku. He ate it very hungrily. And, our operation had begun again. We found each corner of the cargo hold. There was nothing. But while searching, I saw there was something which covered with a black dusty cloth. I removed the cloth, under it were 20 wooden barrels. I opened one barrel and inside it...were weapons! And a square shaped small paper was there as well. Something was written on the paper, but I ignored it and kept in my pocket. There were knives, swords and even revolvers. I opened each barrel to check if there were weapons in every one of them. And there were. I called everyone and showed them the weapons. We one by one took the barrels out from the ship. But it was impossible for us to take all the barrels to the portal together. Because there were 20 barrels and we were just 6! Amar asked "So, how are we gonna get these to the portal?" I replied "I don't know." Kabir suggested "We need a big pull cart." Ria said "Yeah, I know that as well, but from where are we gonna get a pull cart." I removed the piece of paper which I kept in my pocket, if by coincidence it got useful. And it was useful! On the paper it was written:

Join your hands, close your eyes and say the spell written below. Then think of whatever you want in the next 10 seconds and you'll get it. But it will cost you a lot of energy. The spell-

Ka ba ni keken ja!

I joined my hands and then closed my eyes. I spoke the spell "Ka ba ni keken ja!" A pink light started circling me [The others told me about this. I didn't know anything, because my eyes were closed.]. I could feel my body was getting light as a feather. I started floating in the air. But then I remembered about the writings on the piece of paper saying 'Think of whatever you want in the next 10 seconds' and definitely more than 5 seconds had gone. I quickly thought about a pull cart. Suddenly I started feeling very thirsty and tired. The pink light, which was circling around me faded away and I fell down. There was barely any energy remaining in my body to open my eyes. But still I managed to half open my eyes. Everything was a little blur. But I could tell that the pull cart was there. Everyone started asking "Krish, are you okay?' But all the voices faded and my eyes closed. When I opened my eyes, I was fallen in grass. And only looking at the grass, I understood where I was. I was back in Peltica! But I couldn't see anyone around because of the long grass. I stood up and saw behind me. Everyone was there unloading the weapons from the barrels. I quickly ran towards them. I asked Kabir "What had happened to me, Kabir?" He said "That's what I was gonna ask you now; what had happened to you, Krish?" I replied "I don't know." He told me "You read that spell and a pink light started circling you and you started flying in air. And then suddenly, out of nowhere a pull cart appeared. The pink light stopped circling you, then you fell down and drifted into deep sleep. So, we had to take you in the pull cart till here." 'Oh, I didn't know about this. It really happened?' 'Yeah, really.'

CHAPTER SIX

KRISH VS TSARO

{NARRATOR: Ameena}

[Hello, guys! I am back! So, should I start?

Amar: Nope.

Shut up, I'm starting.]

So, as Krish told you everything what happened, I won't repeat it again the way Amar does [Amar: Hey! I don't repeat!

Yeah-yeah. Everyone knows.]

We were unloading the weapons from the barrels. Soon, we were done. Krish and Kabir came walking towards us. They both explained everyone what happened. Krish asked Tsaro "Do you remember what you said, Tsaro?" Tsaro asked "What?" 'Come on, you really don't remember?' 'Sorry, but no.' 'No problem! I'll tell. You said that if someone gave you weapons, you'd give him anything.' 'Oh, yeah! Now I remember. But what about it?' 'We gave you weapons, so you have to give us whatever we say.' 'Oh, okay. Ask, what do you want? Please, don't say 'the whole world'.' 'If I want I can. But I won't.' 'Thanks.' 'It's a very small thing.' 'What?' 'Some food and water.' 'Oh, only this much?' 'Yep!' 'It will be done. We'll give it you while leaving.'

I thought the conversation had ended but no, thanks to Krish. Because he just doesn't tell us his ideas, plans or what he thinks we should do before. He said "What do you mean by 'while leaving'? We are leaving right now." Tsaro said starting an argument "What? You're not gonna help us fight the Rambians." Krish replied "No! We gave you the weapons, now you can fight!" The argument went on for a long time. But when it got interesting was when Tsaro said "If you've got guts come in the red circle." The red circle is a sand filled ground, where fighters battle each other and people bet on them. I don't if it's true or just a myth, but Tsaro told us that the sand's colour before was brown. But by the blood which was shed during the fights mixed up with the sand and its colour changed to *red*.

Everyone started saying "Please Tsaro, don't do it!" But now it was impossible to stop him. The only one who could stop this was Mr. Abelerd. But he had gone out for some important work. So, there was no other way but to let the fight go on.

Tsaro and Krish-both of them entered into the red circle. There were two big screens on the top, where how much amount of money was put on which player was written. Tsaro took his fighting stance. And Krish stood in the normal way. Tsaro said "Let it come!" Krish said as well "Why not." Krish ran towards Tsaro and punched him in the stomach. But from looking at his expression it looked like he didn't feel any pain. Tsaro punched Krish on the left side of his face with his right hand. Krish flew back in air and crashed onto the ground. Spreading sand everywhere. He stood up slowly. Krish's right cheek was swollen a bit. Krish ran towards Tsaro and tried to punch him in the face with his left hand. But Tsaro blocked the attack with his right hand. And then punched Krish in his stomach with his left hand. Krish fell down on his knees. Now a good amount of crowd had gathered around the red circle and, the betting had started as well. There were Rs. 1,069 on Krish and Rs. 1,099 on Tsaro. So, Tsaro was in the lead.

Krish looked towards the screen and saw the amount of money. I guess the money encouraged him to fight. Krish stood up and ran towards Tsaro. He kicked Tsaro in his stomach. Tsaro flew back in air and crashed down. And the next second, the money put on Krish increased to Rs. 1,112! Tsaro got angry. He ran towards Krish and loaded 10 continues punches into his stomach. Krish was hurt.

The fight went on for half an hour.

Both of them were very-very badly hurt. There was a line of blood dripping down Krish's right hand. And his right cheek was swollen a little bit as well. There was a line of blood running down Tsaro's nose.

There was Rs. 2,013 on Krish. And Rs. 1,983 on Tsaro. Now Krish was in the lead. Tsaro ran towards Krish, jumped and kicked his face. He flew in air crashed down badly. Krish stood up and ran towards Tsaro. He punched Tsaro in his face, then kicked him in the stomach and again punched his face. Tsaro fell down, but managed to get up again. Tsaro punched Krish and he slid backwards.

Krish kicked Tsaro's right leg and he fell down on his face. Half of the crowd starting cheering and Krish started showing off. But Tsaro quickly pulled his right leg and Krish fell down as well. This time the other half of the crowd started cheering. Krish tried to get up but his left hand slipped and he again fell down on his face. No one stood up. All the crowd started cheering "Fight! Fight! Fight!" But none of them was able to get up. Tsaro managed to get up. And Krish stood up as well taking Tsaro's support. Tsaro said "I...am...sorry. I shouldn't have got so angry. It's your decision. If you don't want to help fight, it is...okay. No problem." Krish said "No, I'm sorry. I should help." Tsaro asked "Are you sure?" Krish replied "Yes." So, it looked like the fight had ended. Krish was declared as the winner. The money put on Tsaro got added to the money put on Krish. So Krish got Rs. 3,996 in total. We already had Rs. 20,000 and by adding this. It equals to Rs. 23, 996! Krish collected the money and we went to bandage both of them.

We reached at the hospital. The nurses quickly started to make the medicine. And soon we were done. Now we were headed towards the PADHO headquarters. It was something around 6:45 P.M. While on our way, I remembered one thing. I quickly asked "Tsaro, the Rambians were gonna attack us today, right?" He replied "Oh, yeah. You're right Ameena. I forgot about that." Amar asked "It's good or bad?" Sami replied "Of-course, it's good." Amar said "I know that, but the way you said it, it sounded like bad news." Sami said ending the conversation "Oh, no. It isn't."

We reached the headquarters. The second we entered in, everyone started asking 'What happened, how it happened' and all those things. We told them the whole story and they were literally enjoying it. After the explanation ended, everyone went to do their own work. Soon, Mr. Abelerd came as well. He looked at Tsaro and Krish, shocked. He asked "What happened to both of you?" Ria answered "They both fought in the red circle." He asked angrily "What?! Really?!" Ria replied "Yes. It was- *Krish VS Tsaro*!" Mr. Abelerd asked "Are you mad? Why did you fight each other?" We told him everything that happened. He said "Wow, you just fought for this small matter."

Mr. Abelerd went away to do his work. We spent the whole day planning and practicing for the upcoming war.

CHAPTER SEVEN

SURGICAL STRIKE

{NARRATOR: Sami}

[Hello, I'm Sami! And I am gonna narrate this chapter. It feels good to be back.

Krish: I know.

Shut up.

Krish: OK.

So, let's start!]

I woke up the next day. There were no clouds in the sky. The sun was shining brightly. The Rambians hadn't attacked us, at least not till now. We were having our breakfast, thinking about from where to defend ourselves, etc. when Krish shouted "Hey! Why are we thinking of defending ourselves. We can also attack them, right!" Mr. Abelerd said "Right." 'Then what are we waiting for? Let's attack them!' 'Ok, but how? When will we attack them?' 'Today!' 'Not like that. I mean they are alert the in the day.' 'What do you mean in the day?' 'At night they are not alert. Because of the curse of fighting when the moon is visible.' 'Oh, yeah. I forgot.' 'So, we cannot attack them.' 'Actually, we can.' 'When or how?' 'At night.' 'I just said we cannot fight at night because of the moon curse.' 'Have any one from you ever seen someone get cursed? Or have you ever got the curse? How do you know that there is a moon curse?' 'It's written in the ancient books.' 'That's what I'm saying. It is just written in the books, no one has ever been cursed or seen someone get cursed. It can also be a myth. Not everything written in a book is the truth. It can be a myth as well.' 'You can be right. But no one even dares to check if it's a myth or truth. Because everyone is just too scared.' 'So, what? We will check it.' Tsaro interrupted "What? No way. We love our life, and we don't want to lose it." Me and Ameena said "Krish is right. No one has ever got cursed or seen someone get cursed."

Krish asked "What do you think, Mr. Abelerd?" Mr. Abelerd said "Hmm...let me think." He thought for a few minutes. Finally, he replied "Actually, Krish is right. We should go for it." Everyone surprisedly looked at Mr. Abelerd. He continued "Everyone, start the preparations. We're gonna attack them tonight!" Tsaro asked "Sir, really?" Mr. Abelerd nodded. Tsaro said "Ok, start the preparations!" and went away to do some work for the night strike.

I won't waste any time in telling what we did the whole day. Because you would know it already, we practise and planned for the strike. I'll directly start from the night.

We all were ready. Everyone was wearing their armours and were having a weapon in their hands. Mr. Abelerd commanded "I know you all are scared. But we have to do it. And I know, you can do it! Now let's start the '*Surgical Strike*'! Follow me." We all followed him. The moon was smiling in the sky brightly. We had reached theborder of Peltica and Rambia. Mr. Abelerd asked "Everyone ready?" Everyone shouted "Yes, sir!" Krish said "Shoo! Don't shout. The enemy will get awake. They are sleeping now." Tsaro asked "How do you know?" Krish replied "I have a binocular." 'Oh, okay.' Krish said 'Ready,' Everyone gripped their weapons tightly 'Set.' Everyone got in the running stance 'Go!!!' Everyone shouted and ran towards the borders. I'm sure the enemy might have woken up. We all jumped over the borders and entered Rambia. In a few minutes we reached the RADHO headquarters. Its full form is Rambian Attack and Defence Handling Organisation. I had taken a few grenades with me as well. I quickly took out 2 grenades from my bag and threw it towards the headquarter building. And it blasted, breaking the wall. All the Rambians got alert, they quickly woke up and came to defend their country. We had an advantage, because they weren't attacking as it was night. One Rambian came running towards me. I quickly took out a small knife and stabbed it into his stomach and then removed it. He fell down. Two men went running towards Krish. He had a claymore sword. Krish slashed his sword on the both the men's chests. They both fell down. More Rambians came running towards us. But they didn't attack. So, it got easy for us to remove them out of our way. The war went on for 30 minutes. But suddenly one man came running towards me and punched me in the stomach. I kicked him in the face and fell down. I was pretty surprised; how did he attack me. Because they were just defending themselves, not attacking. But soon I knew how he attacked me. Their leader had arrived. When Kabir asked 'What's your name?' and the one who replied 'I am Hatsari, the boss.' came. He was their leader. He commanded "Everyone, don't be afraid! Go and attack them! Nothing will happen!" All the Rambians came running towards us. I quickly took out my slingshot and started finding a sharp rock. I found a few good and sharp rocks. One Rambian came running towards me with a knife in his hand. I aimed for the man's head and let the rubber string go. The rock hit the man's head. I quickly took another rock. And hit one man in the chest. Three men went running towards Kabir. Kabir had two katanas with him. The men went to attack him. But Kabir just did something with his swords and the men fell down. It was so fast; I didn't even understand what he did.

Suddenly, it started showering. But soon it was raining heavily, but no one stopped. The war was still going one. One man was gonna stab a dagger in Ria's back, when Amar shot a dart at the man. The dart hit the man in his neck and he fainted.

Two men went running towards Ameena. She stabbed one end of her sharp-edged stick into the first man. Then she climbed the first man's chest, removed out the stick and jumped on the second man. The first man fell down. And then stabbed the other end in the second man's head and smoothly landed on the ground. Her landing splashed water everywhere. She stood up and removed out the stick from the man's head and he fell down.

There was something kept in a corner, which was covered in a navy-blue coloured sheet. Krish shouted to Kabir "Kabir, quickly come here!" Krish ran towards the sheet-covered thing. Kabir was fighting one Rambian, he kicked the man and he fell down. Kabir quickly ran towards Krish.

Krish pulled the sheet. And inside it was the unthinkable! There...was...a bike! And not a normal bike! It was a ***Motocross Bike***!!! Krish sat in the front, and Kabir at the back. Two Rambians were fallen dead in front of them. There were 2 two-barrelled Lancaster pistols in their hands. They quickly took it from their hands and started the engine. I got busy looking at how were the others fighting. Suddenly, I heard a shout and when I looked towards the direction of the voice, at that time I noticed that four Rambians were coming to attack me. But even before I could move. Krish and Kabir came with full speed towards me and drifted the bike and stopped exactly in between me and the Rambians. Splashing a lot of water on the Rambians. Krish and Kabir took out their guns and aimed for the Rambians heads. Their hands reached the trigger and boom. The bullet shot into the Rambians head. Sprinkling a little bit of blood. They fell down. I said to Krish and Kabir "Thanks for help." They said "Welcome." They both went away to fight the others.

The speed of the motocross bike was full. Suddenly, out of nowhere Hatsari appeared; their leader. He had a water-soaked wooden branch in his hand. Hatsari and they both were just a few centimetres away. Krish and Kabir, both of them were shocked. They were losing control on the bike. When Hatsari hit the centre of the motocross bike with the wooden branch. The wooden branch broke into 2 pieces. The motocross bike skid & they fell down. Splashing water everywhere. The bike went skidding towards a very small wooden warehouse and crashed into it. And the next second, it blasted. Spreading burning wooden pieces everywhere. But the fire quickly went out because of the heavy rain.

Krish somehow managed to get up. His left elbow was bruised a bit. Kabir was still fallen on the ground. Krish slowly started walking towards Hatsari. And soon he started running. Krish punched Hatsari in the face. Nothing happened to him. He punched Krish in the stomach, and Krish fell down. There was a blood-stained dao sword fallen beside Hatsari. He bent down and lifted up the sword. Krish stood up again. Now the rain had started to slow down. Hatsari started walking towards Krish. Hatsari and Krish were now face to face. Krish was very angry right now. Because the fight was just going on for a long time, it wasn't ending at all. And no one was even helping Krish, because we all were just too tired to stand up. Everyone was fallen down on their knees or was sitting down. I was very surprised; it is not at all easy to fight for this long. How was Krish fighting for this long. Oh, sorry, I got bit carried away. So, yeah. Hatsari and Krish were standing face to face. Hatsari tried to hit Krish in the head. But Krish gripped the blade of the sword tightly. Saving his head. By looking at his face, we could understand that he was tired, but as well as angry. It was a pretty easy win for Hatsari, as Krish was tired but he wasn't. At that time, I remembered. While Krish was in the hospital when the bee had stung him. He was reading a book called 'The Magic Spells!' He was telling us about the spells. I quickly shouted to him with all the energy which was remaining in my body "Krish, remember the spells written in 'The Magic Spells!' book! Which you had read at the hospital!" He closed his eyes, I guess for remembering a spell. It had stopped raining by now. Then he opened his eyes, and said "Kraitxin De Fuabuck!" His eyes turned light blue and suddenly the sword blasted. Hatsari flew in air and crashed into a bunch of wooden logs. Quickly all our army ran towards Hatsari and arrested him. I thought now they will take him to the jail and torture him. But instead Mr. Abelerd said "Hatsari, remember. Don't ever try to capture Peltica. Understood?" He didn't reply. Tsaro kicked him in the face with full force. The he replied "Ye-Yes...yes!" Mr. Abelerd continued "Good, now go." He really let Hatsari go! Slowly all the Rambians went to their homes and we went back to Peltica. Celebrating our victory "Victory is ours! We won! Woohoo!" Our legs were paining badly. The village wasn't too far, but the war had drained out all of our energy. So, it felt like we were walking for hours and hours. We were crossing through a sandy road; it was surrounded by dense bushes. Suddenly, we heard a weird noise from the bush on our left side. We all got alert, ready to fight. Who knows what can be there. The bush started shaking, which made a rustling sound. The shaking got faster. There was something big behind it. The noise had gotten pretty loud. It meant that the thing was just behind the bush. The shaking was faster than ever. And something came out. It was very...

CHAPTER EIGHT

Something Came Out. It Was Very...

{NARRATOR: Kabir}

[Hello, I finally got a chapter to narrate. So, I'll start without wasting any of my narrating time.]

So, I was fallen down on the ground, fully wet. There was no energy remaining in my body, so I just didn't get up. But I heard a spell, which Krish said. I looked up to see what was happening. And what I saw was amazing. Krish's eyes turned light blue and suddenly the sword in Hatsari's hand blasted. And he flew- [Sami: Kabir, it's done. I told it. Narrate the next part! We have gone pretty much ahead.

Oh, yeah. Sorry.]

So, I'll skip that part.

[Sorry, but will you tell me from where to start?

Sami: You weren't listening when I was narrating, right?

Um...uh, no.

Sami: Hmm...okay. Start from 'Something came out. It was very...'.

Okay.]

Something came out. It was very...

[What was ahead?

Sami: You!!!

Ouch! Ouch! Ahh! No, sorry!

Sami: See! Read this! You'll understand.

Okay, thanks!]

So, something came out. It was very...cute! Because it was just a small bunny! I don't know how a baby rabbit shook the bush so hardly, but it was just too adorable. We sat down there. For taking rest and playing with the bunny. Tsaro and Ameena found some fruits to eat. This is the advantage of an herbalist, which is your friend. Ameena is a skilled herbalist. She knows everything about plants, fruits and all that greenery thing.

Ameena found some edible fruits, and Tsaro collected them. We all enjoyed the fruit feast. Soon, we were done. We stood up. Our energy had returned a bit. So, we started walking towards our village. The sun was shining brightly! While we were walking, I heard some footsteps behind me. So, I quickly turned back. No one was there, except some footsteps in the sand. Which actually meant someone was there and following us. I quickly alerted everyone. I guess the people who were following us understood that we had found out they were following us so the revealed their identities.

Mr. Abelerd said "Everyone get ready. These are thieves." There were knives in their hands. But they didn't notice that we had bigger and better weapons than them. We all took out our weapons. The second they saw our weapons; they started running away. But we weren't gonna let them escape so easily. I threw the sword in my hand towards one of the thieves. And it hit him in the centre of his back. He fell down. I quickly ran towards the thief whom I hit, and took out the sword stabbed into his back.

Krish ran towards one thief who was running away. He quickly jumped and hit him in the back with his katana. But the thief was strong. He didn't fell down. He turned back towards Krish and tried to hit his head with a small knife in his right hand. Krish blocked the attack with his katana and then punched him in the stomach with his left hand. The knife fell down from the man's hand. Krish quickly slashed his sword into the thief's chest. The man fell down. The tallest and the fattest thief from the thieves' gang tried to attack Tsaro. The thief ran towards Tsaro and tried to punch him. But Tsaro caught the man's hand. And then stabbed his big sword into the fat thief's stomach. The thief groaned. Tsaro took out his sword and he fell down.

Like this one-by-one we all finished the thieves and started walking towards our village.

The energy which we regained through eating the fruits got drained again, as we fought the thieves. We soon reached our village. Firstly, we went towards the hospital and the nurses bandaged us. There were only 25-30 beds in the hospital. And the patients were a lot more than that. So, there was a long line waiting for their chance to get bandaged. We waited until everyone was bandaged and feeling good. In half an hour everyone was done and good. The other men from our army went to their homes.

Me, Ameena, Kabir, Ria, Amar, Sami and Tsaro reached Mr. Abelerd's home. When we reached. Mr. Abelerd told something in Mrs. Abelerd's ear. She smiled and nodded. Then she said something into Mr. Abelerd's ears and went into the kitchen. Mr. Abelerd came and sat down on the chair. We were sitting at the dining table. He looked up towards us and shouted "I know you don't have home or anywhere here to stay. But that doesn't mean you'll always come at my house! The day you came here, you ate at my house. Today again you want to eat at my house! Not expected! And what about you Tsaro? You have a house, right?" Tsaro nodded. Mr. Abelerd continued "Then why have you came to my house?!" Tsaro didn't reply for some time. Then he started "I-" Mr. Abelerd snapped "You all are very bad!" He looked very angry. He stopped shouting. But still, we didn't say anything, just to confirm. Mr. Abelerd didn't say anything. So, we were clear to go. We all stood up together. Mr. Abelerd got surprised. We all said together "Sorry." And walked towards the door. I opened the door.

When Mr. Abelerd started laughing. We all got surprised. We turned back towards Mr. Abelerd. He stopped laughing and then said "Come here! And sit down. I was just joking. Come on!" We all let a sigh of relief. Then started laughing. We all went towards the chair and sat down again. Soon, Mrs. Abelerd came at the dining table. With plates in both of her hands which were full of food. She one-by-one bought plates of food and kept it on the table. There were more than 20 plates on the table. She kept the last plate on the table and said "Children, have as much as you want because this is a special grand feast for you all!" We all shouted excitedly "Yay! Woohoo!" We ate a lot. Our stomachs were too full. We spent the whole day resting and packing all of our things. Because we were gonna leave for the Killer's Pool tomorrow. We packed everything. Tsaro, Mr. Abelerd and the others kept the barrels of food ready for us.

The next day we woke up and quickly got ready. Because we wanted to start our journey as fast as possible. By 11:30 A.M. we were done. They helped us take the barrels till our ship through the portal. We stuffed all the barrels and now, we were ready to go. I had forgot to give Chikimuku food again. I quickly gave him 2 pieces of meat to Chikimuku. And now were done! Krish shouted "Ready to go!" The others shouted "Yes!" The ship started moving. We waved our hands and said "Bye!" to Tsaro and Mr. Abelerd.

Our journey continues! We're back on the road-I mean on the water!

CHAPTER NINE

"3...2...1 AND YOUR TIME STARTS NOW!"

{NARRATOR: Ria}

[Hello, it's Ria there. Finally, we have left Peltica. There are some more adventures coming up. So, I'll start.]

So, we finally have left Peltica. Now I hope we reach the Killer's Pool as fast as possible. We were in the waters. The sun was shining brightly. The wind was going on. The birds were chirping. There were the sound of the waves. It was very calm. We all were relaxed. Drinking orange juice. I took a deep breath and let it go. We were very relaxed. Suddenly, the ship started shaking. The waves weren't calm anymore. A big monster appeared in front of us out of nowhere. Its skin was light pink coloured. That thing had 2 eyes.

[Kabir: What's special in that? Everyone has 2 eyes.

No, I mean some monsters have more eyes.

Kabir: Oh, yeah. Continue.]

It opened its mouth. There were literally more than 10 trillion teeth. It roared loudly. A squishy-squashy slime-like thing fell down on the deck from its mouth. It smelled really bad. I took out my weapon. The bow and arrow. I aimed the arrow towards the monster's left eye. And let it go. It hit the monster and it closed his left eye. He groaned loudly. It started splashing water everywhere. It again roared loudly. It made the front of our ship rise up and the back started drowning into the water. I quickly hung the bow onto my back. The ship started tilting upside-down. We all started sliding towards the back. There was a wooden pole drilled into the wooden board. I quickly grabbed it. All the others grabbed me. We were hanging onto it for minutes. It stopped roaring, then closed its mouth. The front of the ship came down and the back came up. Now we were balanced. I removed my hands from the pole and then stood up. Before we could do anything. It again opened its mouth. Suddenly, it started shooting fireballs towards our ship. One of the fireballs hit our ship's deck. And now our ship was on fire. Our ship was burning! Amar started shouting "Fire! Help! Fire!" Krish said "Shut up! To whom are you calling for help? The monster? Or who? Keep your mouth shut." Amar said "Sorry."

We were trying our best to dodge the fireballs. Our ship was fully on fire. While were running here and there. I spotted a small island a little ahead of us. Suddenly, the floor was feeling slippery. When I looked down, I saw the deck was full of oil. One oil barrel had leaked. So, all the oil was spilled on the floor. I got an idea! I shouted to Krish "Krish, come here! I have an idea." He came running towards me. But when reached near me, he slipped and fell down. I helped him get and then explained him the whole idea. He said "Hmm, it's a good idea!" I explained the idea to the others as well. Krish went to bring Chikimuku. I quickly threw the wooden barrels of food into the water. The others jumped onto the barrels as well. Krish and Chikimuku came running and jumped onto the barrels. They neatly landed onto the barrels like the others. I quickly lifted up the leaking oil barrel which was now, on fire. It was soon gonna blast. I threw it towards the monster. I was gonna jump as well. When I saw a brown coloured pouch fallen on the deck. It was the pouch, in which all of our money was kept. I quickly ran towards it, took it and kept it into my pocket, and then jumped down. I landed safely onto one of the barrels. And the next second. The barrel blasted! And soon the whole ship blasted as well. We were floating on the water. By using our hands, we pushed ourselves towards the island. In 10-15 minutes, we reached the shore of the island. We had lost half of the barrels in the ocean. There was wooden board on the beach. There was something written on the board. It said:

Explocivania

I guess it was the island's name. There were many people enjoying on the sea shore. There was a bar in front of us. We walked towards it. When we entered in, there were many tables. And a lot of people were sitting on it. We slowly went walking towards a table. Everyone started looking towards us in shock. And we knew what was the reason behind it. We had a tiger with us! The table was in a corner. The table and the chair were made up of wood. We sat there. There was a menu card kept on the table. We were thirsty so we decided to order 6 half glasses of Giyakongo. It is an energy drink. We called the man who was taking orders. The man came to our table. He looked very fierce. He was bald and having an eye patch on his left eye. He also had a long beard. There was a small notebook in his left hand and a fountain pen in his left hand. He asked in a rough and loud voice "What do you want?" Krish ordered nervously "Um...uh, six cups-I mean six half glasses of Giyakongo." He shouted nodding his head 'Okay!' and went away. We waited for our order. In 10 minutes, our order came. The waiter kept the glasses in front of each one of us. The Giyakongo's colour is golden. I took one sip of it. It was very good. It tasted like a mixture of strawberry, mango and vanilla. I suddenly started feeling energetic. I finished my glass in just 5 minutes. So, I ordered another one. It was just too good. I called the waiter again to tell him to give another glass. He said "Sorry to interrupt. But if you want more. We have one scheme for you. Wanna try it?" I asked "What is the scheme?" He replied "You'll get a bucket which will be filled with 50 full glasses of Giyakongo. If you finish it within 30 minutes, you'll get everything for free. Everything you have bought and whatever you want to buy. But if you don't, you'll have to pay for the bucket and also whatever you have bought. Wanna try?" I looked at the others. They all said together "No. No way." I nodded with a smile on my face. I said to the waiter "Okay, give me the 50 glasses."

'Okay, madam.'

The waiter went away to bring the bucket. Everyone started shouting on me "Are you mad?! How're we gonna drink 50 full glasses?! Do you even know how big they are?!" Krish said "One half glass of Giyakongo costs Rs. 100. And the full glass costs Rs. 200! If we don't finish it, we have to pay money for all of it. Which'll cost us Rs. 10,000! It will take half of our money. And when we add the bill of our first drink, it will make a total of Rs. 10,600!!!" I said "Calm down. This all will happen only "***if***" we don't finish it. But what if we finish it! Then we'll get everything for free!!!" Ameena said "Yeah, she's right." Everyone said ending the conversation "Hmm...okay." In 10 minutes, the waiter bought the bucket and kept it on the table. He then took out a silver stopwatch. He asked "Are you ready?" We all sat upright and replied "Yes!" He counted "*3...2...1* and your time starts now!" Everyone quickly took out one glass from the bucket for themselves. I took one sip, and I got refreshed a lot! I drank it in one sip. I kept the glass down making a ***thud*** sound. Then took out another glass and then drank it as well. I myself drank 20 glasses. My stomach was full. The others had drunk 20 glasses as well. Still 10 glasses were remaining and we only had 10 minutes. There was no other way, we had to finish it. No one was even drinking a single sip; they were so full. We all drank it, except one of us. Chikimuku! He hadn't drunk it! I don't know if tigers like or drink juices. But still I thought to give it a try. I took out one glass from the bucket and kept in front of Chikimuku. First, he didn't drink it. Then he licked it. And I guess he liked it. Because after that he moved back a bit, shook his head and body. And then started drinking it rapidly. In half a minute, Chikimuku finished the glass. We quickly kept 2 more glasses in front of him. He drank it in 1 minute. Still 7 glasses were remaining. I kept another glass in front of him. But he refused to drink it. So, I forcefully convinced everyone to drink at least one glass. In the next 5 minutes everyone had drank one glass. Still one more glass was remaining. And we only had 2 minutes. I was so full; it was just impossible to drink more. I didn't drink it; I waited a bit to see if I can drink another glass. The waiter alerted "Only 30 seconds are remaining!" I let a loud burp out of my mouth. Suddenly, my stomach started feeling light. I quickly grabbed the glass of Giyakongo and started drinking it. The waiter started counting '3!', five sips of Giyakongo were remaining '2!', three sips of Giyakongo were remaining '1!', one sip remaining. I banged the glass on the table and removed my hand off the glass. The waiter shouted "0!!! Congratulations, you have won! You'll get everything for free!" We all celebrated 'Yay! Woohoo!!! We won!' I asked "Our stomachs are full. We will not buy any more Giyakongo. Now what should we do with the free voucher?" Amar suggested "We can buy bottles of Giyakongo, and drink later on when we want while our journey." Krish said "Yeah, that's a good idea. But where we will keep the bottles?" Amar replied "On our ship! Oh, sorry. I forgot our ship got burned. So, what should we do?" Sami said "I have an idea!" Kabir asked "What?" She explained "We'll tell them that we will buy it later. Then ask if there is a ship dealership or something here. We will go, buy a ship, then come back and buy Giyakongo." Ameena said "Hmm...good. Let's go." We went to the counter. Krish said "We'll buy it later, when we will comeback." But the man at the counter said "Sorry, but if you want to buy anything for free. You'll have to buy it before you get out of the bar. If you go out and then come back, you won't get it for free." Krish said "OK." He turned towards us and asked "What to do?" I said "I think we should buy it and tell them to keep it with them. We'll take it back when we will come back." Kabir said "Good idea." Kabir said "We are buying it now, but keep it with you. When we'll come back, we will take it from you." The man said "Hmm...okay." I guess the man is a fool. As we are getting it for free. Buying it later, or buying it now but keeping it with them and take it later is the same only.

Krish asked "Is there any ship dealership or something like that nearby?" The man on the counter replied "Yes, there is only one." I asked "Where?" He gave us a map and then replied "See this 'X' mark on the map, that's where the ship dealership." Krish took the map from his hand and said "Thanks." We turned towards the exit door. We walked towards it. I started feeling drowsy, my body started feeling heavy. I was feeling sleepy as well. Suddenly, I fell down.

CHAPTER TEN

OPTIMISCU INUDO

{NARRATOR: Ameena/Krish}

[Hello guys, I'm back!

Amar: Shut up!

Why you don't let me talk?

Amar: It makes me sleepy.

Now just stop talking. Let me tell the readers why there is written 'Ameena/Krish' on the top before my timepass talk time ends.

Amar: Ok, continue.

So, you might be wondering why there is written 'Ameena/Krish' on the top. I'll tell you. It's because in this chapter we girls and the boys are both in different places. So, to narrate what happened with both of us, me and Krish have decided to divide this chapter. Oh, now my timepass talk time has ended. I have to start with the story narration.]

AMEENA'S NARRATION-

So, Ria suddenly fell down. Everyone started asking "Are you okay, Ria?! What happened? Are you well?" But she didn't reply. Suddenly, she started snoring. I asked "Hey! She's sleeping now! Come on Ria! We have some important work to do! Just get up now. You can sleep in the new ship, when we'll buy it." Kabir said "She isn't sleeping because she wants to." Sami asked "What does that even mean?" Kabir continued "It is the effect of over drinking Giyakongo. It is making her sleepy. So, she won't wake up until an hour." Krish asked 'Then how are gonna go to buy a ship?" Kabir said "Then, I guess we'll have leave her here." We girls started shouting "What?! No way! We're not gonna keep her here!" Amar asked "Will you carry her all the way to the ship dealership, which is 6 kilometres away." I replied "No." Kabir said "That's the only way." Krish opposed "No, that's not the only way. There is one more way. You girls can stay with her here until we come back." Me and Sami looked at each other. We both nodded, turned towards the boys, sighed and then said "OK, we'll stay here until you come." Krish said ending the conversation "Good, now we should leave." Krish opened the map and they went away walking.

So now we have to wait with 'Sleeping Ria' until the boys come back with the new ship. And we both-I mean we three are gonna get bored until Ria wakes up. I forgot to tell that Chikimuku stayed with us as well.

Ria is the only one who cracks good jokes. Me, Sami, Chikimuku and Sleeping Ria sat outside the bar on the soft sand of the beach, leaning onto the wooden walls of the bar. Cool breeze started coming. The birds chirping, the waves splashing. It was actually a good time.

KRISH'S NARRATION-

[So, hello guys! Ameena has completed her narration part, now it's time for my part. Let's start.]

It's been an hour since we left and still, we have not found the ship dealership. We were walking on a clean road made up of cement. There were big buildings on our right side, and bungalows, apartments on our left side. As of the map, we were just a few metres away. But here, there is not even a trace of that ship dealership. Soon, we reached the 'X' mark which was given on the map. Nothing was there except some trees and plants.

Suddenly, we started hearing noise, someone was hitting wood with a metal hammer. Amar asked "What's that noise? Are you hearing it?" I replied "Yes." Kabir asked "Where is that coming from?" I tried to find from where the noise was coming from by hearing neatly. I found it! I replied "The noise is coming from the right!" The noise was coming from our right side. But there was nothing but just some trees. We started following the noise and went walking into the woods.

The deeper we got into the woods, the louder was the noise. It meant we were getting closer to the source of noise. The trees started getting thinner. The woods started getting less dense. Suddenly, we were in a big open ground. It was as big as a cricket stadium. The ground was sandy. There were some cracks in the ground. When we looked ahead, there was something in the middle of the ground. It looked like a warehouse from far away. But when we went walking near it. We found what we wanted. It was a ship dealership. There were many ships inside. The dealership was packed by 3 ft tall wooden barricades. There was a gap in between the barricade. The gap was big enough to let a ship pass through it. On the start and end of the gaps were two very tall wooden poles. And onto the poles was a metal board, which said:

Optimiscu Inudo Ship Dealership

We entered through the gate. There were hundreds of ships inside. There was an old man, who was hitting a wooden board with a metal hammer. That man was making the noise. We went to him. He stopped hitting and turned towards us. The old man was wearing a blue shirt and pant with a yellow rubber sleeveless jacket, a construction helmet. He was also wearing yellow rubber gloves and shoes. He asked "What do you want?" I replied "A chocolate." He shouted "You won't get a chocolate hear! This is a ship dealership!" I said "Then why are you asking "what do you want?", we are here to buy a ship." Kabir and Amar started laughing. The man shouted "Shut up!" They stopped laughing.

The old man kept the hammer down and then removed his gloves. He said "Hello, I'm Bard. The owner of this dealership." We introduced ourselves as well. He commanded "Follow me. I'll show you some good ships." We followed him as he said to.

There were ships on both of our sides. Some of them were junk metal ships and some were wooden. While walking, I spotted a white ship far away. I ran towards it. It was a magnificent ship. It looked like it was made up of white ceramic. But I don't know if it sails on the water. I called the others near the ship. They came walking. I asked Bard "What's the price of this ship?" Bard replied "Rs. 1,00,000" Kabir started coughing suddenly. He stopped. It was a little bit out of our budget. [Kabir: A bit? Really?] OK, a lot out of our budget. If you don't remember, our budget is Rs. 20,000. We looked at a few more ships. But we didn't get the type of ship we wanted. I said "Now we'll see this final ship, if we like it, we'll buy it. But if we don't like it, we'll go to another dealership." Everyone said "OK." We went to see the last ship in the row. It was actually a pretty good ship. It was the same like our old ship. It was exactly same. Only the quality and colour of the ship was better than the old one. And its cost was Rs. 20,000. Exactly in our budget. Even if it was a single rupee higher, we couldn't buy it. We decided to buy that ship. I paid the price, and now that was our ship.

There was only one problem. How were we gonna take this huge ship through this narrow sandy path for so far away. I asked "How are we gonna take this ship to the beach?" Amar thought a bit and then said "Hey Krish! Do you remember when we had to take the barrels of weapons from the ship to the portal in Peltica. At that time, you said a magic spell. What was that? Whatever it is, you can say that spell." I and Kabir said "Yeah, that's a good idea!" Kabir asked "But do you remember the spell?" I said "Um...no. Let me think." I started thinking. What do you expect will happen? Yeah, you're right. I remembered the spell. I said "Yes! I remember it! The spell! But from that spell we'll only get things. We can't make this teleport." Kabir said 'But in the paper there was written that whatever you want, right?', I nodded 'Then just think that teleport us to the bar. That's it!' Amar said "Hmm...Kabir's right. Ok, let's try." We went to the ship.

I joined my hands, closed my eyes and got ready to speak the spell. I said "Ka ba ni keken ja!" The pink light outlined me again. Everything same started happening. I quickly thought 'Teleport us with the ship to Explocivania's beach, where we drank Giyakongo in the bar'. It felt like I was revolving. It felt like I was gonna puke. Very-very fast wind started crushing my body. Suddenly, it felt like water was splashing on me as well.

Everything stopped suddenly. I opened my eyes. We were on Explocivania's beach, in front of the bar. We were standing on the sand and behind us in the water was our new ship. All the people on the beach started looking at us surprisedly. I guess because we suddenly came out of nowhere. We saw Ameena, Sami, Ria and Chikimuku were sitting in front of the bar. Ria had woken up as well. They were busy talking. I was very surprised because when the last time I had spoken this spell. I had fainted because my all energy had ended. But this time I was feeling normal. I think because of the Giyakongo, it had given us extra energy. We went running towards the girls. They stood up and I thought they'll say the ship is very good. But instead, they started complaining about how much bored they got and all of that. Later, after their complaints ended. They noticed the new ship. They started saying "Wow! The ship's so good! Woohoo!" We started walking back towards the ship. When I remembered we didn't take the Giyakongo from the bar. I stopped and said "Hey, stop! We didn't take the Giyakongo from the bar." The others said "Oh, yeah! We forgot." We turned back towards the bar and went in to take the Giyakongo. I said to the man on the counter "Give us the Giyakongo we had bought before." I think so the man remembered us, because he immediately opened the fridge and took out a big carton filled with 50 bottles of Giyakongo. He handed it to me. I took it and we went walking towards our new ship. There was wooden ladder attached to the ship. We climbed up the ladder. It was very to climb up when there is a tiger under you. Surprisingly, Chikimuku The ship was very good. We started exploring the ship. When Amar shouted from the deck "Hey guys! Come here! I think so we should get out of here." We went running. When I saw, there was large crowd gathered on the beach. Looking at our ship, which had come out of nowhere. Amar was right. Before anyone does anything bad, we should leave from there. I went running into the cabin, where the helm was. The cabin of our new ship was bigger and better. There even was a chair inside. The chair was made up of wood, and there was a leather cushion attached to the chair. I sat down on it. Our new ship even had a motor and still there was a helm. I started the ship and we drove off the island.

So, we were back on our journey with fifty bottles of Giyakongo with a small fridge-we stole a mini fridge from the bar. In our new ship, there were sockets to plug in chargers and etc. I didn't tell you that there even was a living room. Opposite the cabin, there was a room. I went towards it, opened the door of it. That's when I found out about the living room. I don't know how, but it was very cool. Even when it was hot outside.

After enjoying in the living room, we came out and sat near the deck. Sami said to me "Krish, give me the map. So, we can navigate our way to the Killer's Pool." I said "Oh, yeah." And put my right hand into my right pocket to take out the map. I got tense. There was nothing in the pocket. I removed my hand. Then put my left hand into my left pocket. I got even more tense. I asked "Wait a second. Where's the map?"

CHAPTER ELEVEN

WELCOME TO THE TEAM

{NARRATOR: Sami}

[Finally, I got a chapter after a very long break. Yes! So, should I start?

Amar: ...

Wow! Amar, don't you want to say anything like no or shut up. Anything?

Amar: I was eating a burger. ***BURP!!!***Sorry, start now. I won't waste your time.

Really? Yes, good news.

Amar: Shut up.

You?!

Amar: OK, sorry, continue.

Good.]

What was going on? Yeah- I asked "What do you mean by 'where is the map'? You should have it." Krish said "Yeah, I know. But the map is not there." Suddenly, Amar started laughing. Ameena shouted "Shut up, Amar! This is not a time to laugh. This is bad news for us." Amar stopped laughing and said "No, it is not bad news." Kabir asked "What?" Amar asked "Krish, just check your back pockets. Did you check it?" Actually, Amar is right. Krish didn't check his back pockets. He checked his back pockets. There was a paper roll and I knew what it was. He took it out. Krish said "Oh, the map's here." Everyone let a sigh of relief. I commanded "Come on. Now quickly give me the map." Krish said "Oh yes." He was coming to give me the map. Suddenly, a gust of wind came from our left side. The map slipped out of Krish's hand. It went flying towards the water. But still the map was in our reach if we try to catch it. Krish quickly ran towards the deck. He jumped up and kept his right leg on the wooden deck. But instead of stretching his hand ahead, his leg slipped. And he started going down towards the water. The map was falling down in front of Krish like him. He quickly stretched his right hand ahead and caught the map. But he was still falling down. Kabir quickly came running from my back and jumped down as well to catch Krish. He caught Krish's leg. But now they both were falling. We all jumped to catch them. I was still on the deck. I was holding Ria; she was holding Ameena. Ameena was holding Amar. Amar was holding Kabir and Kabir was holding Krish. And at the last. Krish was holding the map. I pulled up everyone with my full power. I manged to pull Ria up on the deck. She was still holding Ameena. Now we both were on the deck. We used our full strength and one-by-one pulled everyone up. Soon, everyone was back on the ship. We were tired a bit, because of that falling event. So, we went and sat on the soft sofa which was in the cool living room. The sofa had red cushions attached to it. It was curved. And between the sofa, in the exact centre was round small wooden table.

Kabir stood up and walked towards the door. He opened the door. Ria asked "Where are you going?" Kabir replied "Wait a minute." He went outside and closed the door.

After a minute, the door opened again. It was Kabir! It wasn't the thing which was exciting. The thing which was exciting was the bottles of Giyakongo in his hand! There were 6 bottles of Giyakongo. He kept one bottle in front of us on the table. I took my bottle and opened its cap. Everyone did the same thing. Everyone said together "Cheers!" and took a sip of it. It felt very good and energetic. I took another sip and just like this the bottle soon finished. I kept the empty bottle on the table. The others had finished their bottles as well.

We had gained our energy back. So, we came outside from the living room and closed the door. I went walking towards the deck. The view was very good. I looked down at the water. It was weird. In front of us was dark blue water and behind us was light blue water. Both the waters were in the centre. We were exactly in the centre of both the waters. And the next second, we were in the dark blue water. I don't know what or why it was like that but I ignored it. Our whole day went peacefully. No attacks on us, no islands on our way. It was a good day.

Soo, I got night. We went in the living room and sleep. We kept our weapons in the living room for emergency. Everyone booked they're on which they were gonna sleep. Krish switched off the lights and everyone closed their eyes.

THE NEXT DAY

The start of the day wasn't any good. We woke up by the noise of someone knocking on the door of the living room. Everyone quickly got up and took the weapons in their hands. Krish went walking towards the door and peeked through the eyehole. He gasped. The sword in his hand fell down. Krish turned back, went walking towards the sofa and sat on it. Everyone started asking "What happened, Krish? Tell us. What did you see?" Krish said only one sentence "See it yourself." Kabir went to see who or what was outside. He gasped as well and sat beside Krish on the sofa. I said "What the heck is happening? Can't you just tell what's outside? I'm going to see it." I peeked through the eyehole. And I understood why Krish and Kabir got so shocked. I gasped as well. There were more than 50 men on our ship. With guns and swords in their hands. They were wearing judogi but instead of white, they were black. Their faces were covered with black masks, helmets and glasses. It looked like they were here to kill us. Amar said "Please, don't do same like Kabir and Krish." I turned back and said "I won't." Ameena asked "What is outside?" I told them what I saw outside. They were shocked as well. Ameena asked "This is not the Morze Craibinsa sea, is it?" I said "Yeah, I didn't check it." I quickly lifted up the map which was fallen down and unrolled it. I did some checking which necessary, but you won't be able to understand because it's too hard. And Ameena was right. We were in the Morze Craibinsa sea! [Ria: Did you tell the readers what is the Morze Craibinsa sea?

Oh, sorry, I didn't.

Ria: Then tell them quickly, you're just talking about it for so long.

Ok, I said sorry. I am telling it.]

The Morze Craibinsa sea has the largest number of diamonds, pearls and all the costly stuff. That's why it is also called 'The Richest Sea'. To get the diamonds and pearls we have to go deep at its bottom. Then do marine mining. But everyone cannot go and do mining there. Only professionals can. Because the others, who aren't professionals, can destroy the diamonds and the others things in there. So, to defend the sea, from anyone who isn't a professional but wants to do mining in the water. There are some people who are trained and then selected to defend the sea. Basically, they are a type of army. They are called Craibins. Some people say that is the reason behind the keeping the sea's name 'Morze Craibinsa'. There are some books in which the Craibins are described, and their images are shown as well.

And the Craibins look the same as the people which we saw right now. They are said to be one of the deadliest forces in the world. This is the reason why everyone was so shocked.

Where was I? Yeah, I checked the map. We were in the Morze Craibinsa sea! I shouted "Guys, we are in the Morze Craibinsa sea!" The people outside, who were Craibins knocked again on the door. But this time it was much louder. Everyone said to me "Shh...!" I said whisperingly "Sorry." Amar asked "What should we do now?" Krish said "What we always do." Amar asked "What?" Krish replied "Fight!", he stood up and lifted up his fallen sword and continued "Now don't say 'Are you mad? How are we gonna fight them?' We have to fight them and we will." I took a deep breath, exhaled it and said "OK, let's do it!"

We all quickly took our fighting stance with the weapons in our hands. Krish went towards the door and kept his hand on the handle. He turned his neck towards and asked "Ready?" We all nodded. Krish opened the door and we all went running outside screaming. We pushed and threw a few of the Craibins away. But soon we were surrounded by them. One of them removed his mask. The man would be in his sixties. But he had big biceps. He said "I'm Bronsan. The leader of the Craibins." Our guess was right! They were Craibins. Bronsan continued "Do you have the marine mining pass?" We replied "What's that?" He took out a card from his pocket and showed us. The card looked like this:

MARINE MINING PASS

Photo

Name: Bronsan Grewcalds

Age: 55

Role: Leader of the Craibins

Has permission to: Enter, cross and do marine mining.

He explained "This is the marine mining pass. If you want to enter, cross or do marine mining in Morze Craibinsa, you need to have this pass. Do you have this?" Ria replied "No." Bronsan said ending the conversation "Then sorry but we'll have to kill you." He went away walking, and now all the swords and guns were aimed at us.

I quickly punched one man. He fell down. Ria kicked another one in his stomach. He crashed onto another Craibin. Amar quickly shot a dart into one man's neck. And the man fell down. Ameena hit stabbed her stick into a man's head and then removed it. And the Craibin fell down. I thought the Craibins were very deadly, but they aren't strong at all. We easily took down a few Craibins. Suddenly, a tall and muscular man came and kicked me in the mouth and I fell down. The same man grabbed Amar's neck and he fell down. Another man punched Kabir in his face. Kabir fell down as well. And the last one, Ria, got hit on her head. So, we all had failed. All the other Craibins quickly tied our hands. The strong man who had hit me and Amar came in walking with a gun in his hand. He aimed at Kabir's head. Kabir closed his eyes. The man's finger was just a few centimetres away from the trigger. When suddenly a sword came out from our back and slashed through the man's chest. We turned back towards the direction from where the sword had come. Someone slowly came out walking from the shadows. It was Krish! It was his plan I guess to hide, and when we're almost gonna die he'll come to help us. He quickly ran towards the man. He jumped over Kabir and removed out the sword from the man's chest. The Craibin fell down. Krish quickly cut the rope tied to Ameena and Kabir's hands. Kabir quickly stood up and took his katana. They both started fighting the other Craibins. While Ameena quickly started untying us. Ameena was untying us when an Craibin escaped Krish and Kabir and came to hit her. Ameena was unaware of the man who was coming to hit her. Ameena untied Amar. He quickly grabbed his dart gun and stood up. The man was almost gonna hit Ameena. But the next second Amar shot a dart into the man's head. He fell down. Ameena said "Thanks." And quickly untied me and Ria.

Ameena untied all of us. We quickly took our weapons and helped Krish and Kabir fight the Craibins. Krish slashed his sword onto a man's chest. The man flew in air and crashed onto another Craibin. Kabir stabbed his katana into one Craibin's stomach. He removed it out and the man fell down. Ameena stabbed one end of her edgy stick into one Craibin's chest. Another man was at her back who was gonna hit her. She quickly turned back and punched the man in his face. The man fell down, she turned back and removed the stick from the Craibin's chest. And he fell down. Ria shot an arrow into one man's head and he fell down. I aimed at one Craibin's head and shot a rock into his head. He fell down.

There was one man behind Amar. He quickly turned back and shot a dart into the man's left side of the chest. The man fainted and fell down.

We finished all the Craibins. We thought we won, but we were wrong. Bronsan came out of nowhere and punched Krish. He fell down. I quickly ran towards Bronsan to kill him, but before I could attack him. He punched me in the stomach and I fell down. It hurt very badly. I wasn't able to stand up. It felt like the punch drained out all of my energy. I could only look up and hope the others kill him. Ria shot an arrow towards Bronsan. But he caught the arrow and crushed it to pieces. All the arrows had ended. So, Ria went running towards Bronsan and jumped to hit his with the bow. But he dodged the attack and punched her in the face. She fell down as well. Amar started continuously firing darts at Bronsan. But he was dodging it easily. Amar didn't notice that Bronsan was coming forwards towards him step by step while dodging the darts. Amar shot one final dart, Bronsan dodged it and then punched Amar in his face. Amar flew in air and crashed onto the door of the living room. Ameena jumped over Bronsan and stabbed her stick into his back. But he quickly turned back and kicked Ameena. She flew in air and crashed onto Krish.

Bronsan removed out the stick which was stabbed into his back and threw it on the ground. He said "Here comes your end."

Suddenly, something jumped out of the water on our left side. It was a boy, who might be our age. There was a bow and arrow in his hand. He shot an arrow into Bronsan's right side of the chest. Bronsan groaned. The boy landed on our ship. He was wet. Water was dripping down his hair. Bronsan shouted angrily "Ahh!!!" He removed out the arrow from his chest and threw it down. He started walking towards the boy. When suddenly one more thing jumped out of the water. It was a girl; she looked like she was the same age the boy. She also had a bow and arrow in her hand. She shot an arrow into Bronsan's left side of the chest. He groaned more loudly. She landed on the ship. She was wet. The boy went running towards Bronsan and jumped on him. He hit Bronsan with his bow. He fell down. They both came walking towards us. We all stood up. Krish asked "Who are you?" The boy replied "I'm Akshay." The girl replied "I'm Divya." Kabir asked "So, why you killed him? And why are you here?" Akshay replied "When you had come to Peltica we saw you and we loved the way you were fighting. That's why we followed you till here. We want to join The Warrior Teens." Ameena asked "You know about the Warrior Teens?" Divya said "Yeah, we know." Akshay asked "So, will you take us with you?" We all looked at each other. I said "We should let the captain decide it. Krish, you decide." Ameena asked "Wait a second. Where is Krish?" We all started looking for Krish. When suddenly we heard a groan. I looked towards Akshay and Divya. Bronsan stood up behind both of them. I thought he died or fainted but he was alive and awake as well. But before Akshay and Divya could notice him. There was wooden board in Bronsan's hand. He was gonna hit them. When we heard a very loud gun shot. The noise of the gun shot came from behind Bronsan. Akshay and Divya got shocked and got away from there. Bronsan fell down. Blood started spilling on the ground. When we looked forward, it was Krish. He shot Bronsan. And guess with which gun. He shot Bronsan with a ***gold-plated Colt 45 Revolver!*** I said to Krish "I thought the gun got burned." Krish said "No, I had only lost it. I found it now."

'Oh, okay'

Some more Craibins jumped out of the water and landed onto our ship. They looked at all the others who were fallen down and they just said "Sorry." And retreated. We gave them the bodies of the Craibins and they left.

Krish said "I loved your cinematic entry." Divya said "Thank you."

Akshay asked again "Can we join the Warrior Teens? We both are doctors, so we'll be helpful." We do need a doctor. So, we added them as well. We explained them everything. Like about our journey, where are we going, about Chikimuku, etc. They said that they think the Killer's Pool is for real as well. I said to Krish "Krish, quickly start the motor. We have to reach the Killer's Pool as fast as possible. We should not waste any more time." Krish said "Yeah, you're right." He went into the cabin and started the motor. Our ship started moving. It's a good to have some new friends.

Soon, it got night and we all went to sleep in the living room. I just want to reach the Killer's Pool as fast as possible and destroy all the Tarmains. I hope we reach soon.

CHAPTER TWELVE

KILL'S CHAPTER ENDS HERE

{NARRATOR: Kabir}

[Hello, guys. I won't say anything like 'I'm back' or 'finally I got a chapter' because it's my work to narrate a chapter when I'll get to.

Ria: Don't try to look smart. I know you want to narrate a chapter too.

Ok, you're right. So, should I start?

Ria: Why not.

Let's start.]

The next morning, I woke up early at 6:00 A.M. The others were asleep. I opened the living room's door and went out. The sun was at the horizon. There was bathroom in the back of the living room. I quickly brushed my teeth, took a bath and came out. The sun was rising. There was a small kitchen in the cargo area. I went down there, kept a slice of meat in front of Chikimuku. He had just woken up. I made some coffee for me. I went up on the deck. There was a small wooden chair, so I sat on it. Drinking the coffee looking at the sunrise. Soon, the others woke up as well. They got ready as well. We made 8 egg omelettes and 8 cups of coffee for breakfast. After eating we were just doing timepass because we had nothing to do. While I was staring at the water, I saw an island a little bit ahead of us. There was smoke coming out from the island. I said to Krish "Krish, drive faster. Take us near that island. I think so there is a fire and someone needs help. We should go and see what's there." Krish nodded and said "Okay, Kabir." Krish drove the ship faster. We soon reached beside the island. The second we reached it. Something blasted and a piece of metal came flying towards me. I quickly ducked down. The metal went towards the other side of the ship and crashed into the water. I stood up and said "Close one." We parked the ship near the island. I forgot to tell that yesterday I found an anchor at the back of our ship. Krish and I put the anchor in the water and one by one went down the ship. There was a big fire in the middle of the island. We had also taken our weapons. We quickly ran towards the centre, where the fire was. When we reached, there was a big open sandy ground. And in the centre of the ground was a metal warehouse or something like that, which was on fire. Beside the burning warehouse were standing some navy officers. Krish quickly ran towards them and we followed him. The navy officers were a little bit bruised. Krish asked one of them "What's going on? How did this happen?" The navy officer asked "Hey! Who're you?" I replied "We're travellers. We were just going by, when we saw some smoke. We thought someone needed help, that's why we came here." The navy officer said "Hello, I'm Officer Arjun." Krish asked "Why aren't stopping this fire? And why are you so hurt?" Officer Arjun replied "We aren't stopping this fire, because we set it on fire. This is the warehouse of Kill." Ameena asked "Who is Kill?" Officer Arjun replied "He is a tobacco dealer. Tobacco is illegal in Nrynain. His men who were working here ran away." I asked "What is Nrynain?" He replied "It is the name of this island." 'Ok, you continue.' 'So, Kill is a tobacco dealer. His real name is Oturan. The navy is trying to catch him from a long time. But he is so powerful and fast that he escapes every time. By now we have got orders to shoot at first sight.' Amar asked "Oh, can we help you kill him?" Krish asked as well "Yeah, can we?" Officer Arjun thought for a second and said "Ok, no problem." First, we put out the fire. Then Officer Arjun took us to the navy headquarters. When we reached, there was a big building which was navy blue in colour. There was a big metal board on the building. Which said:

Nrynain Navy Headquarters (NNH)

We went inside. It was very clean and shiny. There was a small section in the building which was a small hospital. We went there and the nurse and doctors bandaged the officers. In ten minutes, they were done. Officer Arjun and the other officers came out. We went and sat on a white leather couch. Officer Arjun asked "So, how are we gonna catch Oturan?" Ria asked "Can you say Kill instead of O-to-ran? It sounds weird." Officer Arjun said "Ok. So, how're we gonna catch Kill?" Krish thought for a few minutes and then asked "Do we have any radars which can detect smoke or fire?" Officer Arjun replied "Yes, we do." Krish said "Good! Tell everyone to keep an eye on the radar. If you spot any smoke or fire on this island, that's where Kill will be. Because while making tobacco, smoke is emitted through the factories. Then we'll surround that place from all the sides, and then attack them. So, there will be no place for Kill to escape from." Ofc. Arjun said "It's a good idea. Ok, I'll tell them." He went to tell all the other navy men about the plan. The plan was good but not that much. A navy officer can easily make a plan like this. When Ofc. Arjun came back, Krish said "We need to make four troops of men. Each troop will contain 50 men. All the troops will surround the place where smoke or fire will be detected from all four sides. When everyone is ready, we'll attack them." Ofc. Arjun said "Ok." And went to make the troops ready. We spent the whole day looking at the radar and getting ready to attack.

THE NEXT DAY

The next morning, we woke up and got ready quickly, because we will have to go anytime. We had our breakfast as well. It was 11:00 A.M. and there was no sign of smoke. We all were gotten sleepy when suddenly the fire alarm rang. Everyone stood up and looked at the radar. The radar had detected some smoke. We quickly sat in the jeeps and went to the place which was shown on the radar. We were in Troop A. The place was very far away. The road was dusty and full of trees and plants. It took us 20 minutes to reach. When we reached Ofc. Arjun's phone rang. It took it up. The other officer on the call said "Sorry sir, but all the other 2 troops cannot reach there." Ofc. Arjun asked "Why?! What happened?" The officer replied "The tires of our jeeps got punctured." Ofc. Arjun started "But-" the other officer ended the call. I asked "Now what should we do, Officer Arjun?" He replied "Wait." We waited for a long time. 20 minutes were gone by now. When we got a call from the headquarters, the lady on the call said "Sir, the smoke is soon gonna stop. Which means Kill will get away. Have you caught him?" Ofc. Amar replied "No." The lady said "Sir, hurry. This is the moment." And ended the call. Officer Arjun sighed and said "Attack." Amar asked "How are we gonna kill or catch him? He will run away." Ofc. Arjun replied "We have stop him until the other troops come. If we don't even attack, he'll just run away." Amar said "Hmm...you're right. Let's go!" Officer Arjun commanded the other troop to attack as well. We started our jeep and went to attack Kill. We reached a big sandy ground. There was a big factory there. There was a metal board on the factory which said:

KILL'S TOBACCO FACTORY AND DEALERSHIP

We were at the right place. Kill made a big mistake writing that on the board. But it was good for us. Everyone quickly jumped out of the jeeps. All of our men had guns in their hands. Men of Troop B surrounded the factory aimed at the entrance and exit of the factory. Men of Troop A, means we, went near the factory. The men of Kill were big bodybuilders. They were wearing black t-shirt, jeans and black shoes. There were black glasses on their face and AK47 in their hands. We were waiting for Kill to come out. Finally, after ten minutes he came out. He had very big muscles. He looked like a professional bodybuilder. He was wearing a white t-shirt, a golden coloured woollen cloak and black jeans. He was also wearing black glasses. He was talking with a man. I guess he was his customer. One man from Troop B was having a *bazooka*. He aimed at Kill and shot the missile. The missile crashed onto a pillar and blasted. Nothing was visible. There was too much dust and debris. The dust went away. Now it was neatly visible. Kill was standing there. His bodyguards and the customer were fallen down. He was alone. There was dust and sand all over his body. The lenses of his glasses were broken. He removed his glasses and threw it on the ground. He looked very angry. Suddenly, all his men circled him and started firing towards us. We quickly took cover behind a broken wooden log which was fallen near us. The firing stopped. One man from our troop peeked out to see why the firing stopped. No one was there. We stood up and started walking towards the factory. Suddenly, out of nowhere a man came out. There was bazooka in his hand as well. He launched a missile towards us. But before we could take any cover. The missile crashed in front of us on the ground and blasted. We all flew in different-different directions. I tried to stand up but one man of Kill came running towards me and punched me in the face. And I fainted.

When I opened my eyes, I was sitting on my knees in the ground. Beside me was our whole army. Our weapons were kept just behind us. Our hands and legs weren't tied. I don't know why. In front of us was standing Kill. He had changed his clothes. Now he was wearing a white t-shirt, a golden coloured woollen jacket and black jeans. He started laughing and then said in a powerful and clear voice "Hahaha! Trying to kill me. Hahaha! Getting killed yourself." Kill acted a man to bring something. The man came running with an old type wooden gun. He gave it to Kill. Kill took the gun in his left hand and pointed it at Krish's head. He asked "I don't wanna kill you. You're a child. But your behaviour made me do this. It won't pain. Ready?" Krish replied looking at Kill fiercely "Nope, not at all." Kill said "Hmm...brave. Good. Hahaha!" His finger reached the trigger. He was almost gonna shoot, when Krish punched Kill on his chin. His face turned towards the sky. The gun fell out of his hand. Kill quickly punched Krish with his right hand with using his full strength. Krish crashed down on the ground spreading dust and sand. Ofc. Arjun went running towards Kill to punch him. But he dodged it and punched Officer Arjun in his face and he fell down. The other men from our troop started firing at Kill's men. I quickly took my katana and ran towards Kill. I tried to stab the katana in his stomach but he grabbed the blades with his left hand. He snatched the katana from my hand and threw it down. Then punched me in the face with his right hand and I fell down as well. All the men from Troop B jumped on Kill. He fell down on his knees. The men covered him from all sides. We couldn't see him. I thought that finally we stopped him. But the next second all the men flew in different-different directions and crashed down. Kill stood up screaming "Ahh!!!" Ameena, Sami and Ria ran towards Kill. Ameena jumped up on him, but he dodged her attack. He snatched the stick out of her hands. Threw it behind him and punched her in the stomach. She flew in air and crashed down on the ground. Ria aimed Kill's head and shot the arrow. Kill ducked down and the arrow went over him. He stood up and the next second Ria jumped on him to attack with the bow. But he grabbed Ria's neck and threw her away. Sami shot 4-5 rocks continuously at Kill. But he dodged each one of them and kicked Sami in her stomach. She flew away and crashed onto the ground. Amar, who was standing behind Kill, shot a dart into his neck. Kill turned back towards Amar angrily. He removed the dart out of his neck and threw it towards Amar. Amar quickly ducked down and the dart went over him. Amar stood up and the next second Kill punched him in the stomach. Amar fell down. Both-Akshay and Divya continuously shot 20 arrows at Kill. But he just dodged it. Only 1 or 2 arrows hit Kill. Soon, their quivers were empty. All the arrows had ended. Kill quickly ran towards them and grabbed Divya's neck. Then he threw her on Akshay and they both fell down.

When Kill was fighting the others, we all quickly stood up and took our fighting stance. Kill took out a pager and pressed some buttons. All his men came out from the factory with AK47 in their hands and started firing at us. We quickly took cover behind the same wooden log. Suddenly, the firing again stopped. When we saw, Kill was sitting in a red Lamborghini, and all his other men were running away as well. I don't know how a Lamborghini came out of nowhere. We quickly started firing at the Lamborghini. Our troops fired so much that the Lamborghini's tyres lit up on fire. One bullet shot through the car's glass and shot into Kill's right side of the chest. The car crashed into a wooden box which was full of bags of cements.

He opened the door and walked out of the car. Kill started running away. We started firing at him rapidly. 20 bullets shot into his back. But he was still running. Krish quickly started running behind Kill. A helicopter was stood in front of Kill. Kill was almost gonna reach the helicopter, when the helicopter blasted. Kill flew in air and crashed on the ground in front of Krish. When we saw towards the burning helicopter. We saw Troop C and Troop D coming in front of us in the ground. Kill managed to say "Even if I die, my business will continue. My men will sell the tobacco everywhere." And then he closed his eyes. Krish looked towards the factory. He ran inside to catch Kill's men. But they were too much. He turned his neck towards his right side. There was a big tank. Which was open from the top. There was a sticker on the tank, it said 'Oil! Caution! Danger!' Is oil needed to make tobacco? I don't know. So, where was I? Yeah, Krish came out running. He turned his neck towards his left side. There was a wooden ramp, which was covered with hay. He turned his neck towards his right side. Where the Lamborghini was. Its tyres were still on fire.

Krish quickly ran towards the red Lamborghini. He opened the car's door and sat inside. He closed the car's door. Krish drove the Lamborghini towards the ramp with full speed. He drifted and climbed the ramp. The burning tyres of the Lamborghini set the wooden ramp on fire as well. He increased the car's speed even more. The ramp ended and the car flew in air. Krish quickly opened the door and jumped out of the car. He landed down smoothly and got away from the factory. He commanded the others to get away from the factory as well. The Lamborghini crashed inside the oil tank from the opening above it. A little bit oil spilled out of the tank and the next second. ***Boom!***The tank blasted. The whole factory was on fire. Some of Kill's men fled away. Some died. But the tobacco, cigarettes and cigars got burned.

We thought Kill had died. But we were wrong. He was still alive. He was sitting on the ground leaning to square bales of hay. Krish went walking towards Kill. He lifted up the old wooden gun which was fallen down with his right hand and pointed it at left side of Kill's chest. Krish said "Tobacco is really injurious to health." and shot Kill.

He threw away the gun and came back walking towards us. All the navy men started clapping for us-The Warrior Teens. And that's how Kill's chapter ended here. We went back to the navy headquarters and bandaged ourselves there. We slept there for one night and the next day left for our ship. The navy men followed us till our ship to guard us. When we reached, they stood at the island's edge. We one by one climbed up the ship. After climbing up we turned back towards the navy men. We all shouted "Bye!" Krish went into the cabin and started the motor. Our ship started moving and then all the navy officers saluted us together. As we got far and far away from the island. The officers turned back and walked away. We enjoyed fighting Kill. I hope we get someone powerful like Kill at the Killer's Pool to fight. Yeah, but not too much, that even we'll not be able to fight him.

CHAPTER THIRTEEN

A TALKING TIGER!

{NARRATOR: Amar}

[I enjoyed listening to others narration. But the most fun is in narrating by yourself. I know it's hard to get a chapter quickly because we are totally six and two new members are added which means eight. So, everyone needs to get a chapter to narrate. But whenever I get to narrate, I enjoy it. Now I am starting the chapter. Let's go!]

We have left Nree-na-in. [Ameena: It is Nrynain.

Yeah, I know that,]

It is so hard to pronounce, a weird name. So, we have left Nri-nain, no Nrynain. Yes, I got it. And by now everything is going smoothly, nothing has attacked us nor we have spotted an island and went to help the people living there. We were just sitting and enjoying. It was a good day. No one to disturb us. We all were relaxing on the chair or the ground. Krish brought 8 bottles of Giyakongo. He gave 1 bottle to each one of us. Akshay and Divya didn't know what Giyakongo was. Because Akshay asked "What is this?" Krish replied "This is Giyakongo." Divya asked "What's that?" Krish asked "You don't know what Giyakongo is?" They both replied together "Nope." Krish explained "Giyakongo is an energy drink." Akshay and Divya accepted the bottle and said "Oh, thank you." Krish said "Welcome." And sat on a chair. Everyone opened their bottle's caps and started drinking it. They both took a sip. Their expressions were telling that they were surprised and feeling more energetic. Akshay exclaimed "Wow! This thing is really good!" Divya added "Yeah! Very good!" Soon, our bottles ended. We were just relaxing. We didn't have any work. When Sami asked "Hey! Will these much of weapons be enough to fight more than 500 Tarmains? I don't think so." Ameena added "Yeah, we should buy some cannons or something like that." Krish said "Hmm...you're right, we should buy some cannons. But where will we get firearm store?" Sami said "Leave that to me." Krish said "Okay." Sami went to check the map. After 10 minutes she came back and said "It is just a few kilometres away. We'll reach there in half an hour." Krish went into the cabin and the ship was now sailing faster than before.

25 MINUTES LATER

We soon reached there. It was just a small piece of land. There was only 1 shop on the island. It was literally in front of us. If we wanted, we could just shout to the man in the shop to give us some cannons because it was so close. But we wanted to examine the cannons and the weapons we needed to buy neatly. So, we decided to go at the shop. I don't know why but Krish decided to take Chikimuku with us as well. He brought Chikimuku out of the cargo hold and fed him a slice of meat. Chikimuku just finished in just a single minute. We climbed down the ship and went walking towards the shop. The shop was very small and made up of wood. The shop's name was written on a black board which was kept in front of the shop. The board said:

KARAN's Weaponry

(Firearm shop and gun shop)

There were many weapons kept inside and outside of the shop. Big weapons like catapult, cannons, etc were kept outside. And small weapons like guns, grenades, slingshot were kept inside. Krish said to the shopkeeper whose name was Karan, as it was written on the board "Show us some good cannons." Karan had a long beard and wore a black and white cap. He said "Yes, sir." Karan opened the shop's door and came outside. He showed us some cannons.

But after looking at all the cannons only 2 of them were fitting in our budget. So, we decided to buy them. Krish took out the small pouch in which our money was, and poured everything on the counter. Making the pouch empty. Karan gave us both the cannons we had selected. When we reached our ship, suddenly Chikimuku started roaring. Krish managed to get near him. I don't know why was he roaring so much. But Krish knew. Because he said "See Chikimuku's leg!" There was a metal nail stuck in his leg. That's why he was roaring so much. Krish calmed down Chikimuku. He quickly removed the nail. And Chikimuku literally said "Ahh!!! Ouch! It pains so much." By looking at Chikimuku's expression it looked like he had made a big mistake. I asked "Chikimuku, how can you talk?" He just replied! "Uh...yes." Everyone started exclaiming "Wow! Woohoo!" Krish shouted "Shut up!" Everyone stopped shouting. Krish asked "Chikimuku, you can talk. Then why didn't you tell us before?" Chikimuku replied "I just didn't know that should I trust you. But now I can. So, I just spoke." Krish said "Wow. So, should we go back?" Kabir said "Yeah, why not." Chikimuku opposed "Sorry, but I cannot come." Ameena asked "Why?" Chikimuku explained "My parents told me that if you speak in front of any human just come back." Sami asked "But why?" He replied "Even I don't know." Kabir said "Oh." Chikimuku said "If you need me, just speak 'Abronx Caime Dwon!' and remember me. He started walking away and he just vanished. We didn't want him to go, but he had to. It was needed. So, we just let him go. We went neared to the ship.

I asked "How're we gonna take these 2 cannons up there?" Sami replied "By using the spell Krish used for bringing a pull cart out of nowhere in Peltica." Krish opposed "No! We shouldn't use a spell every time. We should first try by ourselves. If it doesn't work, then you should spell and all that magic." Ameena said "Yeah, Krish is right!" Kabir asked "So, how are we gonna take these cannons up there?" That second, I got an idea. I said "I know." Kabir asked "How?" I replied "Half of us will climb up the ship and throw a rope down here. Half of us will stay down here and tie the rope to the cannons. Then who will be up on the ship will pull up the cart." Ria said "Hmm...good idea."

Krish, Kabir, me and Akshay climbed up the ship. We started finding a rope. Finally, I found one rope in the cargo hold where Chikimuku used to live. But now he doesn't. [Ria: Shut up! Don't make it emotional.

Oh, sorry.]

So, I gave the rope to Krish and he threw one end of the rope down the ship. Ameena caught the rope and tied it to the cannon. Me, Krish, Kabir and Akshay pulled up the cannon. It literally took us 10 minutes. It was very heavy. We managed to bring the cannon up on the ship. I pushed the cannon a little back. Then repeated the same process. This time it took even more energy and time to pull up the second cannon. It was very much tiring.

Soon, the girls came back up as well. Krish went in the cabin and started our ship. Now we were back on our journey with 2 cannons.

CHAPTER FOURTEEN

THE FINAL SHOWDOWN-PART I

{NARRATOR: Ameena}

[This is gonna be my last chapter of this book. So, I'll give it my best while narrating.]

We had set the 2 cannons at the deck. So, our journey's gonna end soon-

[Krish: Hey! Don't tell them everything!

Oh, sorry.]

Our journey was going very smoothly. We were enjoying on our ship. When we heard a creature's groan. The noise was coming from the water. We quickly ran towards the deck and saw towards the water. There was pink light glowing under the water. Suddenly, something jumped out and landed on our ship. It was a pink coloured monster. It was small and very-very cute. The creature had 4 legs. The monster groaned again. When we saw towards its leg. We understood why it was groaning. There was a small cut in his paw. Krish commanded to Kabir "Quickly! Bring the first aid box, Kabir!" Kabir went running and quickly came back with the first aid box in his hand. Kabir handed the first aid box to Krish. He kept it on the ground and opened the box. Krish took out an antiseptic liquid bottle and a triangular bandage. He applied a little bit of amount of antiseptic on the wound and then put the bandage. The creature smiled and jumped back into the water. We kept the first aid box away and relaxed again.

But the world just doesn't want us to get relaxed because the next minute I heard a roar. At first, I was unable to recognise what it was. But the next second, I understood. It was the Tarmain's roar!!! I shouted "It is the Tarmain's roar!" Everyone started looking here and there for the Tarmain. But there was no sign of the Tarmain. So, we just sat down again. I thought I got hallucination. But we were wrong. We again heard a Tarmain's roar. I again went to see from where the voice was coming from. What I saw was horrible. There was a whirlpool as big as the Big Ben! And if that is not enough. More than 100 Tarmains were circling the whirlpool. It doesn't end here. We were already getting sucked towards it! I shouted "Everyone! Come here! You need to see this!" Everyone quickly came running to see what happened. They were as shocked as me. Sami asked "What should we do now?!" Amar said "I don't know!" Krish said "Wait! I'll try something." And went into the cabin. Now our ship was going reverse. But still it wasn't enough. We were still getting sucked towards the whirlpool. When suddenly a Tarmain came towards us and hit its head into our ship. We all fell down. Another Tarmain came to attack us. Kabir stood up and punched the Tarmain in his face and it crashed into the water. We all stood up as well. Kabir quickly grabbed his katana. Another Tarmain came to attack us, Kabir quickly jumped on the Tarmain and stabbed his sword into its chest. The Tarmain was moving so fast, that Kabir was gonna fall down. The katana which was stabbed into the Tarmain's chest got out. And Kabir flew in air and crashed onto Amar. The Tarmain fell down into the water. Kabir stood up and went to take his katana, which was a few metres away from him.

Suddenly, another Tarmain came and grabbed Amar's right leg with its mouth. He lifted up Amar and took him into the whirlpool. Krish came out of the cabin running and shouted "Amar! No! I'm coming! Kabir and Ria, go and attack the Tarmains with the cannon." Kabir and Ria said "Okay!" and went towards the cannons. They started firing at the Tarmains. Krish shouted "Amar, I am coming!" and started running towards the deck to jump down. Kabir turned his head towards Krish and said "Krish, stop! Don't act mad." But Krish didn't listen and went running towards the deck. Kabir quickly went running towards Krish. Krish was almost gonna jump, when Kabir caught him, pulled him back and kept down. Krish asked "Why're you stopping me? I have to help Amar!" Kabir shouted "Are you mad?! They'll imprison or kill you as well. Don't go." Krish pushed Kabir and stood up saying "I don't care! I have to help him." He again started running towards the deck. When Kabir quickly lifted up an empty wooden barrel and hit it in Krish's head. The barrel broke to pieces. Krish stood straight for a few seconds, then fell down.

We fought the Tarmains for a while, but they were advancing on us. So, we had to retreat. Kabir took us a little bit far away from the whirlpool and the Tarmains. Everyone was hurt a lot.

In an hour, Krish woke up. We all were sitting on the ground, leaning onto the deck. Krish stood up and started shouting "Hey! Who hit me?!" Kabir replied honestly "I hit you." Krish grabbed Kabir's collar and said "Why did you hit me?! Why you didn't let me help Amar?!" Kabir said "Look! Everyone is hurt! How were they gonna fight more Tarmains or help you? We should not force them to fight. And you weren't stopping from fighting them. That's why I had to hit you. Look at them, how much hurt they are." Krish turned his head towards us. We all were hurt very badly. Krish realized that Kabir was right. He removed his hands off Kabir's collar. Krish apologised "Sorry." And sat down.

We all had bandaged ourselves. Krish asked "When are we gonna go and rescue Amar?" I suggested "We should attack them the next morning because we are very tired. Till tomorrow our energy will get high again." Krish said "Hmm...Ameena is right. So, it's final. We're gonna rescue Amar tomorrow morning." We spent the whole day sleeping, drinking Giyakongo to regain our energy as much as we could.

NEXT DAY MORNING

It had gotten morning. We all were ready. Everyone quickly grabbed their weapons. Krish went into the cabin and we soon reached the whirlpool. I grabbed my stick tightly. We jumped into the water, and we started getting sucked towards the whirlpool. I was just a few centimetres away from the whirlpool. Suddenly, I went inside the whirlpool. Water started getting into my mouth and nose. I was losing my breath. The water was getting stuck in my throat and getting inside my eyes. I closed my eyes quickly. It felt like the water was crushing me. The sound of the water started getting muffled.

Suddenly, all the water disappeared. Everything stopped. I was on an island breathing heavily. There was sand under me. The water was dripping down my hair, nose and mouth. I started coughing a little bit. When I looked up, I front of us, there were a little bit of trees. When I looked beside me, the others were not there. I quickly stood up, stick and started looking here and there, but there was no trace of them. By looking at my surroundings I understood where I was. In The Killer's Pool! Suddenly, I heard some noises from between the trees. So, I walked towards it to see what the noise was of. I thought there were a little bit of trees but it was more than that. I continuously walked straight into the deep trees, dodging venomous insects and plants.

The trees started to get less dense. I was able to see some light so I started running towards it. The trees were getting less and less dense. While running I didn't notice the trees had ended. I was in a plain and big ground so I stopped running. In the centre of the ground was a wooden chair and on the chair was sitting a boy. Our friend, Amar! His hands and legs were tied. There was a tape on his mouth which made him unable to talk. I went running towards him and quickly removed the tape. He shouted "Ow! It hurts!" I apologised "Sorry." He said "Actually, thanks. It feels good, I can talk again." While talking I heard some noise coming from the bushes behind me. I quickly turned back. The bushes were rustling. Someone was there. I lifted up my stick and got ready to fight. The rustling got faster. I gripped the stick more tightly. Someone came out. It was Krish! He came running towards me and asked "Are you okay? I was finding everyone from a long time." I replied "Yes, I'm okay. See I found Amar." Krish asked Amar "What happened after the Tarmain take you into the whirlpool?" Amar replied "The Tarmain grabbed my leg and dragged me into the whirlpool. I went into the whirlpool and water started going into my eyes, nose and mouth. I started getting dizzy and I fainted. When I woke up, I was sitting here. My hands and legs tied, and a tape on my mouth." I asked "That's it." Amar replied "Yep." Suddenly, the bushes on our right started rustling as well. This time I didn't took my fighting stance because I thought the others will be there. But Krish quickly stood in his fighting stance. Someone came out and I was right. It was Akshay, Divya, Sami, Kabir and Ria. They saw us and got very happy. They all quickly came running towards us. I asked Ria, Divya and Sami "Are you okay?" They replied "Yes." Krish asked Akshay and Kabir "Are you okay? How did you find us?" Kabir started "Yes, I'm okay. We j-" Amar snapped "Will you stop taking and untie me?! The ropes are stinging too much!" We apologised "Sorry." And started untying him. We quickly untied Amar. He stood up and started stretching.

Suddenly, 200 men came out walking from the bushes with axe and sickles in their hands. The men were wearing black t-shirt and black jeans. They had big muscles and there was sand on their faces and arms. Few of them came and grabbed our arms. So, we wouldn't escape. We all started moving our hands rapidly so they will let us go.

When one man came out walking from all the men. It looked like he had just bathed. He was wearing a white t-shirt, a long black woollen jacket with golden strips on it; which reached till his knees. Black jeans and black sunglasses. He had a long black beard with grey strips on it which reached till his chest. He also had big muscles. He was coming towards us. There was nothing in his hand. He came and stood in front of Krish. He said "Welcome to the Killer's Pool! My kingdom." Krish asked "Who're you?" The man replied "How rude? Hahaha! I am Dhruv. The maker of the Tarmains." I don't know why, but Krish suddenly shouted "Ahh!!!" and hit Dhruv under his chin. Dhruv's face turned up. He quickly turned towards Krish and punched in the face. All the men removed their hands from our arms. Krish flew in air and crashed onto the ground.

Kabir went to slash his sword in Dhruv's chest. But 2 of Dhruv's men grabbed Kabir's arms. Dhruv acted them to let Kabir go. They removed their hands of Kabir's arms and went away.

Kabir again went to slash his katana in Dhruv's chest, but he dodged Kabir's attack and grabbed his neck. Dhruv lifted Kabir up and threw him on Krish; who had just managed to get up. They both fell down. One man came running towards me with a sickle in his hand. He tried to hit my legs but I jumped up and dodged the attack. I stabbed my stick into his back. Then removed it out and the man fell down. Out of nowhere 2 men came and grabbed both of my hands. I quickly did a backflip and took cover behind the men. Ria came running in front of the 2 men and shot two arrows at a time. Which hit the men in their chest. They both fell down.

Sami shot a rock at Dhruv, but he caught it and threw it back at her. She ducked down and the rock went over her hitting one of Dhruv's men who was standing behind. She stood up, when a man came and kicked her in the stomach. She flew in air and crashed onto Amar. Making both of them fall down. Krish slashed his sword in Dhruv's back. Dhruv turned back and punched Krish. But Krish didn't fall or crashed into something. He just moved a little bit back. Krish went back running towards Dhruv and punched him in the face with his right hand. He was gonna blow another punch when Dhruv kicked Krish in his stomach. Krish fell down. When Kabir came running with a stone in his hand. He jumped high and hit the stone into Dhruv's head. The stone broke into 2 pieces. Dhruv got a little bit angry. He turned back towards Kabir, punched him in the face with his right hand and then kicked Kabir in his stomach. Kabir flew in air and crashed down on the ground.

A line of blood started dripping down Dhruv's head. Dhruv started wobbling and the next second, he fell down. Akshay and Divya went running towards Dhruv and checked him. Krish stood up and asked "Is he alive?" Akshay replied "Yes, but he is unconscious." We all gathered around unconscious Dhruv. One man came running towards Amar's back. Amar quickly lifted up his dart gun and asked, 'What to do about these-' he didn't complete his sentence but shot the man without even looking at him. Then continued 'We're not gonna escape these 200 bodybuilders, are we?' Kabir replied "Yeah, Amar is right. We are not at all gonna escape these 200 muscular men." Krish said "I have an idea!" I asked "What's the idea?" Krish commanded "I need a rope and a gun." I asked "That's it?"

'Yep, that's it!'

Ria asked "But what is the plan?" Krish explained "It's simple! We're gonna tie Dhruv as tight as possible. Then, take him in front of all his men and tell them to surrender and escape from here." Ria said ending the conversation "Hmm...okay."

We all started finding a rope, when Dhruv opened his eyes, groaned, stood up quickly and punched Krish in his face. Krish fell down. We went running towards Dhruv to hit him. Dhruv shouted loudly "Ahh!!!", bent down and punched the ground with his right hand. Some sand and dust spread in air and we flew in air as well. Then crashed down on the ground. Suddenly, one Tarmain came and started spreading flames on us. We jumped from here to there to dodge the fire. The Tarmain spread flames towards me, I jumped towards my right side; where there was no fire. The next second, I jumped on another place where the fire crashed down on the ground. I thought 'Uh...close one.' I noticed one thing that Dhruv was missing. We started finding him but he was nowhere to be seen.

Krish went running towards the Tarmain, he jumped high and stabbed his sword into the Tarmain's stomach. He removed the sword out and quickly jumped down. Krish came walking towards us and behind him the Tarmain fell down. While fighting the Tarmains we spotted Dhruv, so we went behind him. Dhruv was talking to one of his men. He was unaware that we were gonna attack him. Krish quickly went running towards Dhruv and hit him in the head with the broad side of Krish's sword. Dhruv fell down on his knees. We all quickly aimed our weapons towards Dhruv.

The men aimed their weapons towards us. Kabir commanded "Throw your weapons away! Or else we'll kill your boss!" But they didn't listen to us.

Krish said "Dhruv, surrender. This is your end." Dhruv asked with an evil *smile* on his face "Are you sure?" I nodded and replied "Of course! We're sure." He asked again "Are you 100% sure? Does your teammates think the same as well?" We all started looking at each other. When Akshay and Divya threw two smoke bombs towards us and someone hit me. I was unable to see who it was. Someone again hit me, but this time it was harder. It made me unconscious.

CHAPTER FIFTEEN

THE FINAL SHOWDOWN-PART II

{NARRATOR: Krish}

[This is gonna be the last chapter. So, enjoy it as much as you can. So, let's begin the end of this adventure.]

So, someone hit us in the smoke and it made us unconscious. When I woke up, we were sitting down on our knees. I looked beside me; the others were sitting there as well. Our hands and legs were tied. There was a line of blood dripping down my lip and nose. I was very tired. Someone came walking in front of us. It was Dhruv. There was a golden throne kept there. Dhruv sat on it. He asked "How was the twist?" Akshay came out walking from the behind of the throne on the right side. Then Divya came out from the left side. They both stood leaning onto the throne. The others looked at them angrily. I replied "Amazing!" I don't from where but a question struck in Amar's mind. So, he asked curiously "Dhruv, how did you achieve control over these creatures?" "They weren't creatures like this from the start." Dhruv replied. Kabir asked "What the heck do you mean?" Dhruv explained "They weren't creatures like this from the beginning. They used to be humans, who worked at my office. But one day I stole a super stone which would grant me immense power from the company where I used to work. No one was able to find it out. Only these people managed to somehow sneak on me and found out that I had stolen the super power. They told the founder of the company that I stole it and because of that I got suspended. But still secretly I also took the super stone with me. I decided to teach these guys a lesson. One day, when I went out for a walk, I found them. So, I went towards them and gave this curse that they'll become into some monsters and they will be called Tarmains. And from that day they are in my control. Begging me every day to turn them back into humans." Ameena shouted "You're a monster! A merciless monster." Dhruv accepted "Yeah! You are right." Ameena groaned loudly looking at Dhruv angrily. Dhruv said "I'm getting bored. Let's speed this up. Take them to the seashore, kill them and bury them under the water." 6 men came walking out of the shadows. They grabbed our heads and dragged us all the way towards the seashore. Another 4 men came and lifted the throne on which Dhruv was sitting. The trees and plants on our way to the seashore hurt very badly. Dhruv; sitting on the throne, followed us to the seashore. Soon, we reached. The men threw us on the sand. We all sat on our knees. Amar and Kabir were sitting onto my left side. And Ameena, Ria and Sami were sitting onto my right. Dhruv commanded "Kill them." One man came and stood in front of Amar. He lifted up his sword to hit Amar. When Dhruv commanded "Stop! Kill Krish first, the one sitting in the middle. He is the smartest. He can escape anytime. So, kill him the first." The man came walking towards me and stood straight. The man aimed for my head and lifted the sword. He took the sword down to hit my head with full speed. The sword was just a few centimetres away from head.

Suddenly, a bullet shot into the man's head. The man stopped from hitting my head and then fell down. The bullet had come from behind us. We all turned our heads towards the back. One bright white coloured ship was approaching our island. I knew they were on our side. Because there was white coloured flag which was fluttering rapidly. Something was written on the flag in blue colour. It said:

NAVY

We had helped the navy on...what was the island's name? [Amar: It was something from E.

Kabir: Nope. It was from N. Something like Nri-nai-en.

Sami: Yeah! It was Nree-ni-an. No, did I say it wrong?

Ameena: Yeah, you said it wrong. It is Nrynain, understood? Nrynain.

Yeah, got it, Ameena.]

So, we had helped Nrynain's navy to kill 'Kill'. Hahaha. Kill-kill. So, they were here to help us! If you're thinking how they knew we were here. It's because we had said them to put a tracker on our ship and follow us as we're gonna go to the Killer's Pool, we might need help. So, they were following us from a long time. See we are so smart.

Dhruv shouted "Hey! Someone, quickly kill them before the navy arrives!" One man said "OK, sir!" and came to kill us with a gun in his hand.

We turned back towards our front. The aimed at my head. I shouted "No, stop!" When an arrow shot into the left side of the man's chest. The man groaned 'Ouch!' and then fell down. We again saw back. Beside the navy ship, there was another ship. Th e ship was made up of wood and there was something painted on the outside of the ship. It was not a drawing; it was a word. The paint said:

PELTICANS

They were the pelticans. We had helped them fight the Rambians. They were also here to help us. I really don't know how these guys had come here. But whatever it is, it was good for us. A Tarmain came to kill us. It opened its mouth to burn us up. But before it could happen. One small, pink and cute monster came out of the water and burned the Tarmain. There was a small bandage on the cute monster's leg. It was the monster which had gotten hurt and we had helped it. It had come to help us. I said "Thanks." I kept my hands in front of the monster and it burned the ropes. But the next second. One man came running behind the pink monster and threw a net on him. The cute monster got stuck and started groaning. The man took out an axe from his pocket and aimed for the monster's head. I didn't have any weapons. I felt very bad, that I wasn't able to help the kind monster. When I remembered something. A spell! I quickly joined both of my hands and shouted "Abronx Caime Dwon!" A small golden coloured portal opened beside the man. A tiger jumped out of the portal and landed onto the man. Making him fall down. It...was...Chikimuku! The portal closed. Chikimuku was scratching his nails on the man's stomach. I quickly untied my legs and stood up. I went walking towards the cute monster and removed the net; under which it was stuck. The cute monster smiled and started burning the ropes tied to the others hands and legs to free them. Chikimuku came walking towards me. I asked "Hello, how're you?" He replied "Good. How are you?" I replied "Very good." There was a bun on Chikimuku's head. I asked "Hey, what's this bun doing on your head?" He replied "Oh, it's a long story." And shook his head. The bun fell down on the ground. Chikimuku quickly ate it.

The ship of navy and pelticans and reached the seashore. They were coming down the ship. I said to Chikimuku "Ok, you go ahead. I'll be back." I took my sword which was fallen down and went running towards the ships.

I greeted them and said "Now come quickly. We have to kill Dhruv to destroy all the Tarmains." Everyone nodded and went running towards the opposing men. Mr. Abelerd hadn't come but Tsaro had. I asked "Tsaro, how did you know we were here?" Tsaro replied "After you left, Mr. Abelerd told us to follow you and help you as you're gonna go to the Killer's Pool. So, we followed you all the way." I said ending the conversation "Oh, okay"

The ultimate battle had started. One man came to hit me. He tried to punch me in the face but I ducked down. Then stood up again. I kept the sword down and jumped up and hit the man in the head with my elbow. The man fell down. I lifted up my sword again. 4 men went running towards Tsaro to him. One of the men tried to kick Tsaro's legs. But Tsaro jumped high and punched another man. He landed down and hit the man in the face with his elbow. Both the men fell down. The other 2 men came running. But before they could do anything. Tsaro punched both of them in the stomach together with both of his hands. Both the men flew in air and crashed onto an empty wooden barrel which was kept behind them. The wooden barrel broke into pieces. Akshay tried to shoot and arrow towards Ria. But before he could Kabir stabbed his sword into Akshay's stomach and he died. Divya shot an arrow towards Sami. She dodged ger attack and shot a rock into Divya's neck. She died.

I went running towards Dhruv. I kept my sword down and tried the same move again; I jumped high and hit him in the head with my elbow. But nothing happened to him. He kicked me in the stomach and I fell down. I quickly took my sword and went running towards Dhruv again. I hit him in the head with the broad side of my sword. Again, nothing happened to him. He kicked me in the face and I flew in air and crashed onto an empty wooden barrel. Dhruv actioned one of his men to bring him something. The man came running with a sword in his hand. Dhruv lifted up the sword. The man went back running. Dhruv's sword was very big. He stood in his fighting position and actioned me to fight with him. I quickly stood up and went running towards him. I tried to stab my sword into Dhruv's stomach. But he blocked my attack with his sword.

The fight went on for hours and hours. It had started to rain. Everyone was very tired. Our men had already killed Dhruv's men. But they were too much exhausted to help us. One man from the navy still manged to stand up and tried to stab his sword in Dhruv's head. But before he could do his move. Dhruv slashed his sword onto the man's chest. The man fell down. Now it was only me and Dhruv. It was: **Krish vs Dhruv**. I was very tired. Dhruv kicked me and I fell down on my knees. He said "You should die a painful death." He aimed his sword for my head and said a spell "Wang Ta Tashi!" There was a red light swirling his sword. He took his sword up and then down to hit my head. I quickly rolled beside and dodged his attack. Dhruv's sword crashed down on the sand. Something blasted and the sand got burned. He turned towards me. I quickly stood up. By looking at Dhruv's sword, I remembered a spell I had read when I was admitted in Peltica. I took my fighting position and said "Piiruwa Sama!" A blue light started swirling around my sword. We both looked at each other. He came running towards me and I went running towards him. Our swords clashed, making a big explosion. I flew in air and crashed onto a rock. My eyelids were felling heavy. But my mind pushed my body to fight more. I thought 'I have to fight! I have to win!' I stood up. Dhruv was nowhere to be seen. When I turned towards my back to see. He was behind me. He came running towards me, grabbed my neck and threw me with his full strength. I flew in air for a lot of time and then crashed down on the ground. I stood up quickly. I was in front of a type of small cave. The others were fallen down, they were resting.

Dhruv came out of nowhere and kicked me in the stomach. I crashed inside the cave. I stood up. Dhruv came and punched me. I kicked him in the stomach. He went a little bit behind. He came running and punched me in the face, then again kicked me in the stomach. I fell down on my knees. There was a black coloured jacket fallen down near Dhruv's legs. There were 5-10 grenades attached to the jacket.

Dhruv sighted the jacket and gave an evil smile. I said "No. Don't even think about it." He said "Oh no, I thought it. Sorry I have to do it now." He lifted up the jacket. There were strings which were tied to all the pins of the grenades. Which meant if he just pulled out one pin; all the grenades' pins will come out together.

He pulled out the pina and now all the grenades were active. They would blast any moment. Dhruv said "Bye-bye." And started walking towards the exit of the cave. But I quickly stood up, went running towards him and pulled him back. He fell down. I kicked him in the face and then punched in the face. I quickly lifted him up and boom! The grenades blasted!

CHAPTER SIXTEEN

THE SECRET UNVEILS

{NARRATOR: Kabir}

[Krish was joking that he was narrating the last chapter. But actually, this is the last chapter.

Krish: Hey! I wasn't joking. Aarav suddenly added an extra chapter. He had told me that I was gonna narrate the last chapter.

Oh, sorry Krish. Hey, why did you do that, Aarav?

Aarav: Oh, sorry. That chapter was getting too long so I needed to add one more chapter.

Oh, okay. So, I'll start.]

The cave blasted. It was a very big explosion. We all went running towards the cave. Nothing was visible. There was only smoke and fire. Everyone started crying except for me. They started walking away crying. I was gonna turn back as well. When I heard someone coughing from inside the cave. I stopped for a second. I saw someone inside. But the smoke covered his face. A cold shiver went down my spine. I thought 'Is it Krish, or is it Dhruv? If it's Dhruv, we all are doomed.'

Someone came out. I shouted "Everyone! He is alive!" Everyone turned back and asked "Who?" I replied "Dh...Krish!" They all came running. Krish was filled dust. We all hugged him. We all clapped for him. Ameena asked "How did you survive this big explosion?" Krish replied "The sand inside the cave was very soft, so I quickly dug a small hole and squeezed myself into it. Then covered the top with Dhruv. He had a big muscular body so like this I survived." Amar exclaimed "Everyone see that." All the Tarmains which were inside the water as well as on the ground got turned into humans. Except for the ones who got killed. All the Tarmain-humans looked around and I guess they understood that we saved them. All the people there started clapping for us.

1 MONTH LATER

It had been a month since we destroyed-I mean saved all the humans who were turned into Tarmains. Our island-Anybo had advanced a lot. There were a lot of buildings. Each building had minimally 50 floors. We were enjoying on the rooftop of a building which had 70 floors. There was a café on the rooftop of the building. Its name was:

BYSON TRYSON CAFÉ

We were sitting around a round table drinking cold coffee. Krish had went somewhere for his work. We were enjoying when we heard a growl. We looked in front of us. There stood an ogre behind Amar. We all looked at it in shock. Amar unknown of what stood behind him asked "What happened? Why're you looking at me like that?" Sami stammered "L-oo-k behind y-you." He turned behind and shouted "Ah!!!" The ogre punched Amar in the face. Amar flew in air and fell down the building. When Krish came running and stabbed his sword into the ogre's back. He didn't stop, he went running and jumped down as well. Krish caught Amar's hand.

The ogre fell down on its knees, then on his face. I don't know from where but Ameena got a rope and went running towards them. She threw one end of the rope down towards Krish. He quickly caught the rope. We all helped her pull them up. They came up. Amar said to Krish "Thank you." Krish asked "But from where did this ogre came?" I replied "I don't know." Ameena shouted "Guys! Quickly come here!" We quickly went to the edge of the rooftop. The view we saw was horrible. There were millions of ogres destroying the island. All the buildings and shops were blasted. There was smoke and fire everywhere. Dark and gloomy clouds were rising towards us.

I guess this is the end. We have got another problem to solve.

So, bye-bye, I hope we meet again soon.

THE

END!!!

About The Author

Aarav Waghmare is an imaginative 11-year-old writer who discovered a love for storytelling at an early age. This is his first book, born from his fascination with fantasy and adventure and a desire to bring vivid worlds and characters to life.When not writing, Aarav enjoys reading books and drawing. A proud dreamer from India, he hopes to inspire other young creators to follow their passion for storytelling.Aarav believes that every story, no matter how big or small, has the power to ignite imaginations and connect hearts. This debut work marks the beginning of what he hopes will be a lifelong journey of creativity, fantasy and adventure.

www.ingramcontent.com/pod-product-compliance
Lightning Source LLC
LaVergne TN
LVHW041128150826
845673LV00007B/2218

* 9 7 9 8 8 9 6 7 3 6 4 7 9 *